PRAISE FOR M. L. BUCHMAN

Tom Clancy fans open to a strong female lead will clamor for more.

— *DRONE*, PUBLISHERS WEEKLY

Superb!

— *DRONE*, BOOKLIST STARRED REVIEW

The best military thriller I've read in a very long time. Love the female characters.

— *DRONE*, SHELDON MCARTHUR, FOUNDER OF THE MYSTERY BOOKSTORE, LA

A fabulous soaring thriller.

— *TAKE OVER AT MIDNIGHT*, MIDWEST BOOK REVIEW

Meticulously researched, hard-hitting, and suspenseful.

— *PURE HEAT*, PUBLISHERS WEEKLY, STARRED REVIEW

Expert technical details abound, as do realistic military missions with superb imagery that will have readers feeling as if they are right there in the midst and on the edges of their seats.

— Light Up the Night, RT Reviews, 4 1/2 stars

Buchman has catapulted his way to the top tier of my favorite authors.

— Fresh Fiction

Nonstop action that will keep readers on the edge of their seats.

— Take Over at Midnight, Library Journal

M L. Buchman's ability to keep the reader right in the middle of the action is amazing.

— Long and Short Reviews

The only thing you'll ask yourself is, "When does the next one come out?"

— Wait Until Midnight, RT Reviews, 4 stars

The first...of (a) stellar, long-running (military) romantic suspense series.

— *THE NIGHT IS MINE*, BOOKLIST, "THE 20 BEST ROMANTIC SUSPENSE NOVELS: MODERN MASTERPIECES"

I knew the books would be good, but I didn't realize how good.

— NIGHT STALKERS SERIES, KIRKUS REVIEWS

Buchman mixes adrenalin-spiking battles and brusque military jargon with a sensitive approach.

— PUBLISHERS WEEKLY

13 times "Top Pick of the Month"

— NIGHT OWL REVIEWS

THE COMPLETE DELTA FORCE SHOOTERS

A MILITARY ROMANTIC SUSPENSE STORY COLLECTION

M. L. BUCHMAN

Buchman Bookworks

Copyright 2020 Matthew Lieber Buchman

All titles were previously published separately by Buchman Bookworks, Inc.. All introductions are new to this collection.

All rights reserved.

This book, or parts thereof, may not be reproduced in any form without permission from the author.

Receive a free book and discover more by this author at: www.mlbuchman.com

Cover images:

Silhouette of military sniper with sniper rifle at sunset © kaninstudio | Depositphotos

SIGN UP FOR M. L. BUCHMAN'S NEWSLETTER TODAY

and receive:
Release News
Free Short Stories
a Free Book

Get your free book today. Do it now.
free-book.mlbuchman.com

Other works by M. L. Buchman: *(* - also in audio)*

Thrillers

Dead Chef
Swap Out!
One Chef!
Two Chef!

Miranda Chase
*Drone**
*Thunderbolt**
*Condor**

Romantic Suspense

Delta Force
*Target Engaged**
*Heart Strike**
*Wild Justice**
*Midnight Trust**

Firehawks
MAIN FLIGHT
Pure Heat
Full Blaze
*Hot Point**
*Flash of Fire**
Wild Fire
SMOKEJUMPERS
*Wildfire at Dawn**
*Wildfire at Larch Creek**
*Wildfire on the Skagit**

The Night Stalkers
MAIN FLIGHT
The Night Is Mine
I Own the Dawn
Wait Until Dark
Take Over at Midnight
Light Up the Night
Bring On the Dusk
By Break of Day

AND THE NAVY
Christmas at Steel Beach
Christmas at Peleliu Cove
WHITE HOUSE HOLIDAY
*Daniel's Christmas**
*Frank's Independence Day**
*Peter's Christmas**
*Zachary's Christmas**
*Roy's Independence Day**
*Damien's Christmas**
5E
Target of the Heart
Target Lock on Love
Target of Mine
Target of One's Own

Shadow Force: Psi
*At the Slightest Sound**
*At the Quietest Word**

White House Protection Force
*Off the Leash**
*On Your Mark**
*In the Weeds**

Contemporary Romance

Eagle Cove
Return to Eagle Cove
Recipe for Eagle Cove
Longing for Eagle Cove
Keepsake for Eagle Cove

Henderson's Ranch
*Nathan's Big Sky**
*Big Sky, Loyal Heart**
*Big Sky Dog Whisperer**

Love Abroad
Heart of the Cotswolds: England
Path of Love: Cinque Terre, Italy

Other works by M. L. Buchman:

Contemporary Romance (cont)

Where Dreams
Where Dreams are Born
Where Dreams Reside
Where Dreams Are of Christmas
Where Dreams Unfold
Where Dreams Are Written

Science Fiction / Fantasy

Deities Anonymous
Cookbook from Hell: Reheated
Saviors 101

Single Titles
The Nara Reaction
Monk's Maze
the Me and Elsie Chronicles

Non-Fiction

Strategies for Success
Managing Your Inner Artist/Writer
*Estate Planning for Authors**
Character Voice
Narrate and Record Your Own
*Audiobook**

Short Story Series by M. L. Buchman:

Romantic Suspense

Delta Force
Delta Force

Firehawks
The Firehawks Lookouts
The Firehawks Hotshots
The Firebirds

The Night Stalkers
The Night Stalkers
The Night Stalkers 5E
The Night Stalkers CSAR
The Night Stalkers Wedding Stories

US Coast Guard
US Coast Guard

White House Protection Force
White House Protection Force

Contemporary Romance

Eagle Cove
Eagle Cove

Henderson's Ranch
*Henderson's Ranch**

Where Dreams
Where Dreams

Thrillers

Dead Chef
Dead Chef

Science Fiction / Fantasy

Deities Anonymous
Deities Anonymous

Other
The Future Night Stalkers
Single Titles

CONTENTS

ABOUT THIS BOOK

Join M. L. Buchman for this five-story collection about the snipers of the elite Delta Force.

Praise for M. L.'s Delta Force series:

- *"The contemporary standard bearer of military romance."*
- *"Top 10 Romance of the Year."*
- *"A romantic adrenaline junkie's kind of book."*

M. L. will lead you through each story with brand-new introductions, their origins, and why they were written.

Discover tales of danger, adventure, and ever-lasting love with the top fighters anywhere.

Five great reads for one amazing price.

INTRODUCTION

I started writing about Delta Force in 2008 when Colonel Michael Gibson stepped onto the scene in an early draft of *The Night Is Mine* (The Night Stalkers #1). It was easy to become intrigued by these unconventional warriors.

They were unconventional in every way.

In a military built around massive, highly structured elements (especially in the 1970s), the 1st Special Forces Operational Detachment-Delta was structured around very small teams. They replaced force with speed, intense planning with intense training, and military convention with operating way outside any envelope ever seen outside the British SAS that they were based on.

For years, the US military fought against using Delta's capabilities, but in our changing world and its changing wars, Delta proved that counter terrorism was far from their only strength. Their ability to react effectively on "no notice" situations turned them into the stiletto in a military built around battle-hammer thinking.

I became fascinated.

These were the warrior elite that every other military unit either aspires to or fears down to their boots.

I've written many Delta Force novels and stories, trying to bring a civilian's understanding to their motivations and their lives. They may be the most elite fighters in any military, but they are still people. It is easy to label such forces simply as "other."

Years ago, I had a couple beers and a lot of fiery-hot Buffalo wings at the actual Anchor Bar where they were created. The friend who took me there talked about how being a cop (and his wife's role as a nurse) made them "other."

"No matter who we meet, at a party or in the grocery store, they see us as outside their society. We aren't treated as people; we're treated as 'cop' and 'nurse'."

It would take me a decade to find where to tell that story. I thought it would be when writing about the elite helicopter pilots of the 160th SOAR Night Stalkers. But it was Delta Force who were the ultimate extreme warriors. And it was in telling their stories that I found a place to explore "otherness."

As to why these five stories for this collection; Delta Force serves many roles within their elite niche. And this expanded far beyond their original counter-terrorism mandate.

One of those roles is that they're perhaps the best snipers anywhere. There are others, the US Marine Corps Scout Sniper comes easily to mind, but the tiny Delta Force (of perhaps 1,200 operators) annually shoots more rounds than all of the US Marine Corps (182,000 personnel) combined.

Practice may not make perfect, but it sure helps.

Most estimates state that a US military action fires between ten- and fifty-thousand rounds per kill. (Some reports place that number as high as a quarter-million.)

Delta Force is estimated to have a shot-to-kill on the scale of five to ten (not thousand, just five to ten). And that includes the fact that they prefer to use three rounds per target as extra insurance.

But the other part of being a sniper, and the biggest impact on the one former sniper I spoke with, was that a sniper sees their target. It's often not a battle. It's not a firefight. They choose a target, see them, in extreme cases may get to know a great deal about them, and then they kill that individual.

All of these factors combined into the telling of these stories. I wanted to look at what drove these shooters to be able to do that. And how did it affect them.

In these five romance tales, I hope that I also have come even a little bit close to capturing that for you.

SOUND OF HER WARRIOR HEART

Delta Force operator Katrina Melman's hearing goes missing when her mission gets blown away. But she's Delta, the Army doesn't pay her to fail.

Sergeant Tomas Gallagher, the best soldier she's ever met, only speaks to her in sharp commanding tones. Now she can't hear him at all.

Only together can they complete the mission if they hope to find the Sound of Her Warrior Heart.

INTRODUCTION

This story was born out of a curious debate with a friend, *just how many nations are there in the world?*

You would think this was a very straightforward question. Yes, it might change with time as one country is annexed or another breaks free, but it's a known number.

Except it isn't.

The UN states there are 193 countries and two "observer states" (Vatican City and Palestine). According to a 2019 article by Stratfor, there are:

- five more that have been recognized by at least one UN member
- three to six others that are self-declared countries
- 206 nations eligible for the Olympics
- 211 who can compete in the FIFA soccer World Cup
- 249 on the ISO Standards list (you know, CH, JP, NZ, US, UK, etc.)

One of the self-declared countries that is only recognized by three other non-UN countries is Transnistria. The UN classifies it as a part of Moldova; it lies between that country and Ukraine. They declared independence in 1990, which everyone around them declared was invalid, but neither was any action ever taken to reannex them.

So I had my setting, a strange little landlocked slice of a country. Their culture and heritage is very Russian, quite distinct from Moldova's Romanian roots. Perhaps Moldova doesn't want them back.

Because I write so much about aircraft and airports, that led me to their tiny, archaic air force, marooned at their lone, non-functioning airport.

But it also led me to another setting that I discovered they had in Transnistria. Six years earlier, I had greatly enjoyed writing in *Where Dreams Are Born* about a vineyard. In the months before this story, I had also written the Delta Force #3 novel *Wild Justice,* in which my heroine owns a vineyard that they visit in the middle of the book.

Here was a chance to return to these two lovely settings, but in a quite different fashion—in battle.

The final element that shaped this tale came from myself. Even with hearing aids, I don't hear terribly well. I've often thought about what would happen if I were to totally lose my hearing.

I gave that challenge to my heroine warrior, and there I opened the story.

1

Purple.

A purple so deep that it made her think of the purest fresh-pressed grape juice.

Purple grapes. Round globes of color so dark that they ate the brilliant sunlight until they were almost black.

Green leaves. Impossibly blue sky.

Katrina knew something was wrong, but it took her a moment to identify what was missing.

Birds. There should be birdsong. Her family's vineyard was never quiet when the grapes were so close to harvest. This late in the season the bees had moved on to more flowery pastures, but the birds should be singing, arguing, playing.

Funny, she didn't recognize this row of vines, she thought she knew them all.

It was hard to care, though. She'd always loved to lie on the rich soil between the rows of vines and stare at the deeply blue sky. She rarely spent that time thinking about the future or the past. In her memories it hadn't been about some boy either. Of course when the boys came along, she'd spent less time alone in the vineyard watching the sky. No, the vineyard was always about the present moment.

A thread of black smoke slid across the blue sky. Burning a slash pile? Too early in the season for that. The summer was still hot and dry.

She reached a hand up through the silence to pluck a grape. They looked ripe enough that half the cluster might fall into her palm at the lightest touch.

Except she didn't recognize the hand. They weren't her slender teenage fingers. Where was the silver thumb ring that Granny had given her at twelve that had finally moved to her middle finger at fourteen?

This hand was strong, with a shooter's callus on the webbing between thumb and forefinger. And why was the hand, *her hand* covered in red, sticky...blood?

A face intervened between her and her view of sky, grape leaves, hand...blood?

It was a hard, male face.

One that needed a shave.

It should have alarmed her that he was so close, but she knew him. Or thought she should. He wore a close-fitting military helmet and anti-glare glasses. She flexed her jaw and could feel the familiar pressure of the strap of her own helmet. Squinching her nose revealed that she too wore sunglasses.

Why did they need helmets to lie in the vineyard to watch the grapes ripen in the sunshine? She didn't like sunglasses, they changed the color of the blue sky. She tried looking around the edges, but they were wraparound, just like his.

He was familiar.

Very familiar.

But never from this close. That wasn't normal.

His lips were moving, but she couldn't hear a thing. "What?"

He clamped a hard hand over her mouth and his lips made a "Shh!" shape, but she couldn't hear anything.

She studied his lips.

Words. They were forming words.

Kat! Are you okay? Not Katrina. Kat wasn't a family nickname. Always her full name in the Melman family. Miss Katrina to the Mexican field hands as if her family were lords and ladies rather than third-generation Oregon vineyard owners.

Sure she was okay. Though it was weird to have the face asking it silently, especially that face. She associated it with a cold, emotionless tone that could slice concrete.

But why wouldn't she be okay? She was lying in a lovely vineyard, the sun warming her face while she watched purple grapes, blue sky, and black smoke from a slash pile fire. It was expanding though. Maybe the fire was out of control.

The bloody hand was still bothering her.

And the silence.

Maybe she wasn't okay.

Maybe she'd been—

The memory slammed in like the blast of a mortar.

Which was exactly what had happened.

2

———

Sergeant Katrina Melman suddenly remembered the feeling of flying.

There had been the high whistle of an incoming mortar round. She and Tomas—who she always teased about abandoning his name's poor H somewhere along the way, cruelly leaving it to wander the world on its own —had dropped flat in the vineyard and offered up a quick prayer for the round to land somewhere else.

It had partially worked. Rather than a direct hit, the force of the blast had merely thrown her aside, slamming her into a line of grape vines. The burnt sulfur smell of exploded TNT overwhelmed the sweet grapes and rich soil.

Pain was starting to report in. Abused muscles, the nasty gash on her hand, but nothing felt broken.

"I think I'm okay."

Tomas shushed her again. Again she had to concentrate on his lips to figure out which words he was speaking silently. *You're shouting.*

"I am?"

Again the hand clamped over her mouth.

The silence. The echoing silence. The world hadn't gone quiet. Her hearing had gone instead.

Deaf.

When she nodded her understanding, Tomas eased off his hold on her. He mouthed out some long sentence that she had no hope of unraveling, especially as he kept looking away to scan the vineyard, hiding his mouth in the process.

"I can't hear you," she tried to make it a whisper.

Tomas spun back to face her and winced.

Unable to hear herself, she'd lost all calibration of her volume.

You can't? Tomas' lips moved, but she heard nothing —not even the proverbial pin. At least she was fairly sure that's what he'd said. Lipreading was something they taught undercover types. She was a shooter.

Katrina stuck with just shaking her head.

Shit! No problem reading that. With quick rough hands he began inspecting her.

She slapped his hands aside then sat up, and wished she hadn't. Every muscle screamed—silently—in protest. She began inspecting herself. Everything moved when she tried it. A quick pat-down revealed no sources of blood other than her hand.

Tomas bound that quickly enough, using the medkit that hung from his vest.

Armored vest.

Field.

Mortar.

She looked around and spotted her rifle tangled in one of the grapevines. She slid it out and it appeared none the worse for having been blown up.

"That makes one of us who's okay," she whispered to her baby. The MK21 Precision Sniper Rifle was fifty-two inches and eighteen pounds of silent death that let her "reach out and touch someone" over a mile away. It was her reason for being—her role in Delta Force. Her role in—

Moldova. She and her rifle had been blown up in a vineyard in the Eastern European country sandwiched between Ukraine and Romania. Except no one was supposed to know they were here. They—

Tomas slammed her down to the ground and lay on top of her and her rifle. She could feel by the rigidity of his body that he wasn't dead. He was bracing over her like a human shield. For half a moment she thought she finally saw a bird flying across the sky. A falcon swooping on its prey. An...incoming round!

She felt the ground buck against her back from the explosion. The air blast hit against the far side of the vines, peppering the two of them with hundreds of grapes blown off the vines. The vintner was going to be furious.

Tomas pushed back to kneeling beside her.

We've... but Tomas turned away and she missed the rest of his sentence. It was as if he didn't want to look at her after lying full length upon her a moment before. They were both wearing combat vests, making it one of the unsexiest moments ever, but she got the feeling he was still embarrassed by it.

Sitting up, she grabbed the helmet straps on either side of his jaw and turned him back to face her.

"What did you say?" Katrina struggled to keep it soft. Tomas didn't reprimand her so she must have succeeded. "I'm deaf."

His eyes widened briefly. Then he grabbed her head, his powerful hands strong but gentle along her cheeks, and turned it to either side to inspect her ears.

No blood, his lips formed the words quickly, but she hoped she got it right.

She heaved out a sigh of relief at his words. Good. That was good. No dribbling blood meant that maybe her eardrums were still intact.

He made a sharp slicing motion to the west with a flat hand. Right. They needed to get moving. He signaled reminders to stay low and go down the center of the path —jostling a vine might give away their changing position.

At her nod, he led off.

Stepping out, she walked straight into a grapevine.

She scooted to the middle of the path and tried again.

This time she plunged into the grapes the next row over.

It wasn't vertigo, she'd had that induced during training and learned how to fire through it. Besides, vertigo always made you spin in the same direction. With her ears out of operation, her balance was off.

Tomas grabbed her arm and, though it felt like he was pulling her hard to the right, they progressed straight down the aisle of dirt between two rows of green leaves with her weaving like a drunkard.

Fifteen seconds later she felt the air thump against

her back as a mortar killed the poor grapevines she'd stumbled into. Whoever was firing at them was good.

3

———

By the end of the row, she began to get a feel for how to counteract her balance problems.

Tomas yanked her down to the soil, scanning the terrain ahead. He might be a hardcore pain in the ass, but she couldn't ask for a better soldier to be at her side. There was no better man to be in a tight situation with in Delta. She'd tried to talk to him in camp, but he always gave her the cold shoulder, with a voice that could be used to chill a meat locker. However, on assignment, he guarded her like a mother hen or big brother. He was the best soldier, and she'd always been drawn to the best, but for some reason he wouldn't even give her the time of day once they were back in a green zone.

That green zone felt awfully far away at the moment.

They lay together at the edge of the lush vineyard. Looking back she could see that it swooped down into a valley and up the next hill in neat and orderly rows. She'd never had a Moldovan wine and wondered if they were any good. Simply by the size of the field, they were successful. She plucked a grape. Blue-purple. Thick skin that resisted her bite before it popped, flooding her mouth with a high sugar content. Merlot probably. Or maybe a Zinfandel, they tasted a lot alike while still in the grape. She could be lying in the hills of Oregon's Willamette Valley…if it weren't for someone firing a mortar at them. Very few mortars being fired in the Willamette Valley in her experience.

Right! Time to start thinking like a soldier again.

Ahead lay a five-meter strip of rough dirt thick with tractor tire tracks. Beyond it lay a field of thin brown stalks she didn't quite recognize chopped off at one meter high. It was a no-man's land in which they'd be completely exposed. Past several hundred meters of stalks, a line of trees.

Tomas tapped her arm and pointed to the right.

Katrina had to scoot forward to see around him. A large red combine was parked in the middle of the field, at the edge of the tall stubble. Beyond it stood sunflowers —acres of sunflowers. Their heads were dried to a gray-brown and the combine would soon be harvesting them. Except the cab was empty and the door hung open. The machine still vibrated and smoke swirled up out of its exhaust stack. The farmer had abandoned his vehicle when the shelling had started.

"I hate working with foreign military."

Tomas nodded his agreement.

That's what must have happened. Moldova was way down the list on the international index of governmental corruption—their score was in the bottom third and falling fast. You could buy the entire parliament for the price of a Super Bowl commercial. Throw in a signed football and you could probably buy the military as well, though she couldn't imagine why anyone would want to.

The US must have dutifully informed someone of their planned operation on Moldovan soil, who had then reported it directly to the Russians who coveted Moldovan territory. Or perhaps she and Tomas were still alive because some faction of the local military had decided to take care of the problem themselves—it wasn't like the Russians to miss quite so many times.

Well, killing a pair of Delta Force operators wasn't all that easy either.

"Where are they?" she asked Tomas quietly. There were two scenarios: the people firing the mortar could see their position, or the mortar crew were hunkered down, out of sight, but had a spotter who could. Either way she and Tomas had to find them.

Tomas pulled out a small radio scanner. In moments he had a lock on the enemy's frequency. She could see by the indicator light that they were real talkers, either locals or overconfident Russians. He hooked up a small DF loop and began rotating it to get their direction.

She tried to remember how she'd been lying on the ground when she'd seen the incoming round. It had come from...the line of trees to the west.

Tomas pointed in two places: one toward the trees, one...in the direction of the combine.

Katrina slid the caps off the ends of her rifle's scope. She tapped Tomas' shoulder. He turned to her and she made as if to press her hand flat against the ground, then repeated the motion on his shoulder.

He lay flat, braced his elbows wide so that he was steadier than the Rock of Gibraltar. Then he rested his head on his folded hands, but turned toward her rather than the combine. Dark eyes. She could feel his dark eyes watching her despite the lenses he wore. They have always watched her, the sole woman on their squad. Every time she turned, Tomas' eyes were tracking her.

Ignoring that, she unfolded the bipod on the front of her weapon and rested it against the small of his back. The combine was parked a thousand meters away and upslope from them so she needed the extra height to brace her weapon. She lined up with a break in the vines and began inspecting the combine at high magnification.

The main harvester bar was set a meter high and she could see its cutters still working. The high cab was indeed empty. The unloading pipe was swung back out of the way. The...

She swung back to inspect the cab. It was empty. But through the double layer of glass, windshield and side window, she could just make out a man standing behind the cab. It was an almost impossible shot, especially for a single shooter. She would have to break the windshield, then the side window, and then might have a chance of hitting the target if he hadn't already moved. Two shots minimum, probably three.

Tracking upward, seeking any way in, she spotted just what she needed. Between the top of the cab and some other piece of gear, a pair of binoculars inspected the vineyard. She flipped off the safety, glanced at the grapevines to estimate the wind—it was so strange not to hear it rustling the leaves—and compensated for the bullet's fall and a thousand meters of windage.

The MK21 had a silencer, but there was always some noise. Now, for her, it was truly silent as it kicked her in the shoulder. A half second later, the binoculars were gone. Between the combine's tires she could see a body plummet onto the field. She worked the bolt and fed another round into the downed spotter just to be sure, not that a .338 Lapua Magnum round would have left much of his head. Even at over a half-mile out, the body twitched from the massive kinetic impact of the bullet. No question that the spotter for the mortar team was permanently out of commission.

There was a whiff of burnt gunpowder as she chambered another round.

She glanced at Tomas and nodded that it was done, but froze halfway through.

He was smiling at her. It was gone the moment she'd caught him at it, but she knew she'd seen it. Tomas didn't smile at anybody for any reason.

No. That wasn't right. She'd seen his smile before— never directed at her, of course—but she'd seen it. But his face, when he smiled, made it possible to imagine Tomas speaking to her in a warm and gentle tone. *That* was too strange for words so she kept her silence.

4

Clearing out the mortar team didn't take long. Idiot One sprang up to go check on the shooter. Idiot Two raced away in plain view and earned himself a shot in the back though he was closer to a mile away by the time Tomas pointed him out.

Katrina busted up the mortar tube and defused the remaining ammo while Tomas hid the bodies. He showed her the spotter's arm tattoo—a black bat hovering over a blue circle meant to represent the Earth. It was a Spetsnaz tat, Russian Special Forces. So, their enemies this morning were one Russian and two locals, because a Spetsnaz would never run from a fight. Spetsnaz. It was a surprise that she and Tomas survived. Definitely time to go.

Her feet were now steady enough that she probably could have navigated on her own, but Tomas showed no inclination to let go of his grip on her upper arm and she wasn't complaining.

There was a steadiness to him. Not merely his gait,

but his reliability. His grip never varied, except to tighten briefly when she stumbled on a particularly gnarly root. He scanned ahead as they moved through the woods.

Last night's insertion into Moldova had been screwed up in a bazillion different ways. The mortar attack counted as a bazillion-and-one.

First, the transport helo had a mechanical failure. A team of mechanics had raced to fix it deep into the night. So, their launch window at dusk had, well, gone out the window. They'd finally hit the ground in eastern Moldova at two a.m. But their ride had long since given up and vanished into the darkness. No option left but to cover the ground on foot, dressed in full US military gear, with much of the transit in broad daylight.

That's why they'd ducked into the vineyard in the first place, good cover. Into a vineyard—and straight into a trap.

Tomas set a ground-eating pace through the woods that they could both maintain for hours with only minimal breaks. Once they were deep in the woods and several kilometers from the dead mortar team, they made quick work of cutting down some wild cherry branches and creating a small lean-to using the massive trunk of a fallen oak. It was several feet larger around than the Willamette oaks, it must be an English oak. She'd always wanted to go walking among the Cotswolds of England and see some of them. Now she was being hunted across the Moldovan countryside. It sure wasn't the same.

Inside their shelter, Tomas called up to Command during a satellite overflight. She couldn't lipread a word because he held the radio so close to his mouth. Whatever their conversation was, it was short.

Katrina focused on picking the small wild cherries off the roof of their bower for them to eat. Tart! But good.

That's when the fact of her deafness slammed home and stole her breath away. What if it wasn't temporary? At first she hadn't had time to think about it, then she'd shoved aside her fear by convincing herself it was just a TTS, a temporary threshold shift. But what if it wasn't? What if—

Tomas tapped her on the shoulder and she almost cried out in shock.

He eyed her carefully, making a point to mouth his question slowly, *You okay?*

So not. But she gave him a nod that was a total lie.

He snapped his fingers close by her ears.

She could only shake her head.

In answer, Tomas reached out and pulled her against his chest. It was awkward; all of the gear on their vests kept it from being close and she had a fistful of cherries, but still she appreciated it. For a moment she lay her cheek against the cool metal of the emergency lifting ring on the front of his vest, and let herself be held.

Making sense of that was no easier than making sense of her deafness.

A woman in Delta Force did *not* let herself be held. She didn't dare let herself be seen as weak, not for a millisecond. Women were too rare a breed in Special Operations and especially in the heavy-duty combat units.

Beyond that, the last person on the planet she'd ever

expect to have empathy was Sergeant Tomas Gallagher—the toughest damn bastard in anyone's army. It was easy to remember his cold, hard voice. But she couldn't reconcile that with the way he was taking care of her.

He held her until she felt some sense of control come back. Not relief. Not hope. But at least the sense that somehow or other she'd get through this and that maybe, just maybe, she wasn't going to be alone in that effort.

She sat up and patted his arm in thanks. It was a good arm, thick with muscle, honed with thousands of hours of training and hundreds of missions. She realized she needed to make herself stop patting him.

Distraction needed.

Katrina passed him a handful of the tart cherries after making clear he had to spit out the cherry pits—they were naturally laced with cyanide. Then she pointed at the sky, to where the satellite antenna had been aimed and made a questioning face.

You can talk, Tomas admonished her. *Soft-ly.* He was over-accentuating his lip movement which helped. Tomas Gallagher being thoughtful was another shock.

She shrugged at her descent into sign language. Not being able to hear immersed her into a strange world of silence that she felt reluctant to break. Also, her own voice was wrong—foreign, muted to silence by whatever was happening in her ears. She could feel that she was speaking, but couldn't hear it, neither volume nor tone.

He tapped the lapel of his shirt, pointed again to the west, tapped his watch, and gave a thumbs up. Command had reported that their targets, a Russian general and a

Moldovan one, were still expected to be in position at the time previously reported.

Good news. The mission wasn't blown yet despite the problems they'd encountered.

He pointed upward, held up three fingers, then placed his hands palm to palm against his own cheek before closing his eyes.

She didn't get it.

He began slapping his pockets but pencil and paper weren't something you carried on a self-contained mission into a "friendly" foreign country. He looked around again, then spotted something.

He held his hand palm up and moved it until he was almost touching her breast. He did it fast enough that she jolted back against the log.

Tomas held up a hand in apology and, if she didn't know better, she'd say he blushed.

This time he moved his palm more slowly until it was suddenly filled with the bright light of a sunbeam that had found its way down through the forest canopy and into their hastily assembled hideout. It had been shining against her ribcage. He tapped his palm, then pointed upward.

"Oh, the sun."

He nodded. This time the three fingers, a tap of his watch, and a sign to sleep made sense. Three hours to sunset when it would be time to move out; she *should* get some sleep.

Tapping his own chest, he made the signal for lookout—a hand shading his eyes.

She held up two fingers, then bent one in half.

Oh, she could speak.

"Hour and a half, then it's my turn to watch."

He nodded and she settled herself more comfortably against the log. A Special Ops soldier could sleep anywhere: a roaring plane flight, inside a bunker during a firefight—didn't matter. Their small shelter was cozy. It smelled of fresh cherries that matched the vivid taste on her tongue and crispy-dry oak leaves. And was very, very quiet.

She sighed.

Then she remembered what it had felt like to be held by Tomas. They were shoulder to shoulder. He had good shoulders.

After a night and a day on the go, she was exhausted.

She leaned her head onto his shoulder and felt him jolt in surprise. It was a long time before his arm settled as lightly as the sunlight on her shoulders. She didn't stay awake long enough to feel whether or not his fingers wrapped around her arm.

5

Katrina awoke with a start. It was soft twilight. She listened carefully, but didn't hear a thing...because, shit, she was deaf. This was definitely going to take some getting used to.

She was also warm and comfortable inside the curve of a man's arm. Of Tomas Gallagher's arm. For a moment she let herself revel in the feel of it, the security of being held, of lying against a man she trusted with her very life.

Except they were both soldiers.

As she pushed herself upright, he eased his arm off her shoulders.

"You didn't wake me for my half of the watch."

He shrugged.

She thumped the side of a fist against his shoulder.

He tapped his ear and then hers with a soft touch.

Oh right, she couldn't listen. "Sorry. I hope you didn't mind me sleeping on you."

He clamped both hands around his own throat and pretended he was gagging.

She clamped a hand over her mouth to suppress the laugh and wondered where the hell Sergeant Tomas Gallagher had gone. The man she knew had absolutely no sense of humor.

"You're being nice to me."

He shrugged and looked down to rummage through his kit for some energy bars. She didn't take the one he offered.

"Why?"

He turned away but stopped when she rested a palm on his cheek. Without his sunglasses, his dark eyes bored into hers. She tried to say something, she truly did, but her throat was suddenly dry.

"Why, Tomas?" finally creaked out of her throat.

He rested one of his big hands over where hers still touched his cheek.

The light was making it harder to see, but he might have said, *I'm an idiot.*

A moment later he leaned forward and kissed her. It wasn't some tentative little peck. It wasn't a question either. It was a kiss that demanded attention. It was hard, fast, and deep. He grabbed either side of her armored vest by the armholes and hauled her into his lap.

Tomas' strength was overwhelming, pinning her against him. She knew that at the least hesitation on her part, he'd let her go, but no hesitation came from anywhere inside her.

Surprise? *Hell yeah!*

Hesitation? *Hell no!* Not from a kiss like the one he was delivering.

In the same unit? *Don't give a shit!*

On a mission? The mission could wait just a goddamn minute—she was busy here. Busy having her rocketing heartrate pound against her chest, if not her ears.

He let her go at last and some small bit of her sanity returned. She was straddling his lap, her arms locked around his neck. One of his hands had slipped down between her armor and butt.

And he was grinning like the big bad wolf.

"You're not a bit sorry, are you?"

He patted his free hand downward to remind her to watch her voice. His other hand was still occupied elsewhere. He shook his head.

"Odd. Neither am I."

She couldn't hear his groan, but she could feel it conducting through her fingertips. He said something that she couldn't begin to follow, especially with the last of the light.

Katrina could only shrug.

He dug his fingers hard into her bottom one last time, pulling her tight against him, vest to vest.

Yep! Her body was screaming for it too, but...

"Mission time," she kept it soft.

He nodded and they tried to disentangle themselves. Somehow one of her pockets of .338 Lapua Magnum magazines got hooked on his spare 7.62mm magazines for the HK416 combat rifle he carried and it took them a moment to move apart.

Once separated, she became terribly self conscious. They *were* on a mission. They *were* in the same squad. And Tomas Gallagher hated having a woman in The Unit —that much she was sure of. Except now she wasn't.

Had he been avoiding her for other reasons than she'd thought?

Duh! So if *why* wasn't the right question, the next question was…"How long?" She tapped his chest then hers to make it clear what she was asking.

He held up a single finger.

"One hour? One day?"

He made a flipping motion.

"Day One?"

He nodded.

"You wanted to kiss me since the first day I joined The Unit? Why?" *Now* "why" was the right question.

He rolled his eyes at her. He tapped her on the chest and held up a single finger again.

"Because I'm the only woman on the team?"

No. He tapped her chest—directly on the sniper rifle magazines that had just tangled them up. Then on the MK21 before he tried a double thumbs up. *You best. Very sexy,* he mouthed carefully. He ran his hand down her vest's side plates, over her ribs, waist, and hips to make his point.

"Because I shoot well? That's exactly what every woman wants to be admired for," despite her words it *did* mean a lot.

In answer he ran a knuckle over her cheek so gently that she couldn't help closing her eyes.

"Okay, not just because I shoot well."

He nodded with a grin. Then he dug out his night-vision goggles and clipped them onto his helmet.

"You are a mystery to me, Mr. Tomas Gallagher."

He gave her a thumbs up and another one of those

killer smiles once she had her own NVGs in place and turned on.

6

Seven hours hard hiking to reach their target point and three more hours to investigate possible hides.

Command had, of course, done their usual head game. That told them that the CIA was calling the shots on this one because they never did anything straightforward if they could do it bass-ackwards instead.

Katrina decided that it was a good thing she'd been in the Army for long enough to know that they *always* did that. At least it made it so that she was only royally pissed rather than in a murderous rage when the truth came out.

When Tomas reported that they were on site, Command informed them that it was the *Moldovan* general who was their target. He was the only person who'd been told about their mission at all. The fact that they'd been attacked by Russian Special Forces had served to confirm that he could be easily bought.

The Moldovan prime minister himself had told his general that the secrecy of this operation was a matter of

Moldovan National Security. Yet here that general was, meeting with a Russian general at a base just over the Moldovan border in Transnistria.

Transnistria was a breakaway region of Moldova, aligned with the Russians rather than the US, NATO, and the EU. Only three other nations recognized it, though it had been a splinter nation since 1992. A splinter the Russians wanted to exploit. Re-annexing Moldova, just as they had the Crimea, would help secure the Russian frontier against an attack by land forces.

Nobody in the West was in favor of that, except the purchased general. The prime minister of Moldova couldn't be seen to act against his own military despite his general's other war crimes, but it was time for a message to be sent.

And apparently it was up to her and Tomas to send it.

As part of the plan, she'd brought a second barrel and bolt for her rifle, and ammunition to match. In less than two minutes she'd changed from the far-reaching hammer of the .338 Lapua to an odd cartridge only ever used in Russia, a 5.45x39mm. It fired only half the distance forcing them to find a location that was both well hidden and close to the meeting site.

Tiraspol airport was technically non-operational, despite being the only airport in the splinter country and housing all five planes of their air force. No one was sure if they could fly, or survive taking off on the aged runway even if they did work.

But helicopters could land here just fine.

It was finding suitable cover that was the issue. They had to get close, preferably well under five hundred meters with such small caliber ammunition, and yet not be found after she took the shot.

Tomas led her in. The airport was unlit except for a single streetlight near the entrance. The runway itself was open to the surrounding farmland, making it easy to walk onto the airfield. They lay in the unmown grass at one end of the runway and inspected the structures carefully.

He tapped his radio, then pointed at the only decent building left standing.

"Command says that's where the meeting will be?"

Tomas nodded.

She studied it through her rifle's night scope and shook her head. Not a chance from here.

Tomas grinned and tapped his temple.

Katrina gestured for him to lead on.

Sticking to a dry drainage ditch behind the buildings, they crossed behind the old terminal and slipped up to the remains of the Transnistrian Air Force. Five Antonov transport planes, all with flat tires—none operational. A dozen helicopters, only two of which looked serviceable, and a pair of Yak two-seat trainers that must date back to World War II. One was clearly being scrapped for parts, but the other one looked serviceable. It was long, an olive-drab green, and had one of those humped glass canopies.

She shook her head.

He tapped the side of the plane.

She shook her head again.

Tomas pointed at the office building.

Three hundred meters away, an ideal shot.

"This is your idea of an exfiltration plan after we're done here? An ancient airplane that may not fly? I'd like to survive this mission."

In answer, he leaned in and kissed her lightly. Apparently he wanted to survive it as well. How was she supposed to argue with how his lightest touch could make her feel?

7

———

Katrina awaited her moment. She was slouched in the front seat of the Yak-18. It smelled of old pilot sweat, gasoline, and sausages. At the moment she was not appreciating her heightened awareness of her sense of smell since going deaf.

Tomas—slouched in the pilot's seat behind her—had inspected and prepped the plane, encouraged at finding the gas tanks full. Then they'd nudged the tail around until she had a perfect shot through the partially open canopy. There would be no sign of where the shot had come from. No one would look in the middle of the airfield. And if someone did, Tomas was confident he could get the plane moving quickly.

The meeting happened as planned. At noon, a brand-new Kamov Ka-62 Executive transport helicopter flew in and landed exactly where expected. It was met within minutes by two cars that had swept in through the front gate.

Tomas knew that if he needed her attention, he could

thump a fist on the side of the airframe from his position in the rear pilot's seat behind her. But for now, her attention was narrowing. It was Tomas' job to make sure that she stayed safe. It was her job to erase the man who had set a trap for her, stolen her hearing, and betrayed his prime minister.

She couldn't kill the Moldovan general outright, or they'd know there was a sniper on the field, but she had a plan.

First to emerge were a half-dozen guards from either side. Then the two generals climbed out of their respective craft at the same moment and approached each other. A Transnistrian official, also resplendent in his uniform, accompanied the Moldovan. It was too perfect.

The guards formed a wide circle facing outwards, thankfully none quite facing their aircraft—even with the flash suppressor, her shot wouldn't be invisible.

The windsock was rippling hard, ten mile-an-hour crosswind, gusting to twenty. Thankfully, she had fired a few thousand rounds of the 5.45mm ammunition at the Fort Bragg firing range to familiarize herself with its flight characteristics—the wind was going to drag this round a long way sideways in three hundred meters. It would make her shot look as if it was coming from well to the west of their current position if someone noticed the angle of attack.

The two generals approached one another, with the Moldovan facing her but not yet blocked by the Russian.

Three shots at two targets. If she was shooting as a Delta, she'd use four, but the Russians fought differently.

When the generals were two steps apart, she fired a single round into the Moldovan's heart. Delta would have placed two there.

On her next heartbeat—in his face. It caught him before he was over the surprise of the first shot.

For the last shot, she picked a Russian guard standing behind the Russian general and put a round through the meat of his thigh.

At his scream, the Russian general yanked out his sidearm as he spun. He then shot the first Transnistrian guard he spotted. In moments, all of the Transnitrian locals were gunned down—including the high-ranking official.

Someone must have forewarned the police—at least enough so as to make them station a team nearby. They swarmed out of the office building and had the Russian general, his troops, and the helicopter pilot under arrest within moments.

Katrina eased her weapon back in through the plane's canopy and waited, but no one so much as looked in their direction. Who would attack from the middle of their own airfield when the perpetrator was so obviously caught red-handed?

The Russians were going to have very poor relations with Transnistria for some time to come.

And Delta? They'd never been here at all.

8

———

"CAN'T WE JUST WALK OUT?" KATRINA WAVED PAST THE canopy at the deserted airfield. Darkness had come and shrouded the only signs of what had happened today: bloodstains on the sun-bleached pavement and an abandoned Russian helicopter.

It was awkward, twisting in her seat to see Tomas' lips with her NVGs. He said something that she couldn't follow.

"What?"

Trust me, accompanied by one of his smiles. She'd learned about them. They were full of promises—ones that she hoped, no, that she *knew* he would keep. It made him impossible to argue with. She just wished that she could imagine his voice as anything other than harsh and cold, but it was all she'd ever heard from him.

She turned back in her seat and tightened the cross-shoulder harness.

"Why walk when you can fly?" She finally worked out that was what he'd said.

She'd had the mandatory basic training and could survive as pilot in a half-dozen different aircraft—*survive.* Her only hope was that his skills were far more practiced than her own. Thankfully, the Yak-18 was a trainer: pilot in the rear, student in the front. It meant she didn't have to touch anything.

No one bothered them as the engine caught and spun to life on the darkened airfield. It shook the plane, momentarily filling the cabin with the acrid bite of exhaust fumes but, at least to her, it was painfully silent.

Tomas taxied them to the blacked-out runway. Then, unleashing a mighty vibration that she assumed was accompanied by a massive roar, the single engine awoke and pulled them down the abandoned runway. The plane jounced and wobbled, but they were aloft before it could shatter her spine.

Once in the air, Tomas turned them south with a confidence she knew she lacked. Safe in his care. Safe in his arms.

The irony wasn't lost on her for a moment. Tomas' very careful attempts to not treat her differently, to not show her his feelings, had only served to enhance them.

She now understood his prior silences. And those in turn had made her more aware of him. It had made her notice what a standout soldier he was. And their distance had probably driven him even harder to excel, which had only made her notice him all the more.

Yet she'd already been deaf the first time he demonstrated his feelings. Even if the damage was permanent, there was no questioning the truth of them— not of the man who had thrown himself over her so that the mortar might somehow kill him but spare her, and not of the man who now flew the old Yak from close behind her.

A half hour later, they slid out of the sky and landed on a long sandy beach. The plane jolted, but not too badly. As always, Tomas knew exactly what he was doing.

They sat together on the sandy shore of a Romanian park along the Black Sea. Small waves broke on the sand in clean white lines as they watched the night together. Tomas had radioed for a helicopter from an American helicopter carrier that was cruising offshore. It would pick them up soon—and drag the old plane out to sink in the depths of the Black Sea erasing the last evidence of anyone interfering at Tiraspol. Now it would just be a plane gone missing, perhaps stolen by an escaped Russian guard, on a much more newsworthy day.

They sat close, hip to hip on the sand.

"What if my hearing doesn't come back?" Their NVGs were pushed back on their helmets, so she might as well have been talking to herself. She wouldn't be able to read any reply on his lips.

But she wasn't alone. He pulled her tight against his side and kissed her on the temple.

Not alone.

She'd always been alone. The family's black sheep, the first one *ever* to enter military service. One of the first women to qualify for front-line combat. Again one of the first into Delta Force. Delta had accepted her, even welcomed her, but she'd been the only woman on her team. It was a lonely existence.

Tomas continued to hold her close. Rather than going

for the kiss, that she would have gladly welcomed, he somehow knew she needed something else even more. Instead, he just held her.

The fear began to slide away.

The fear of the mission—always there during but already fading fast, as usual.

The fear of not being good enough to be a woman in Delta. Even if it was her final mission today, she'd proven that she belonged.

The unrealized terror that she'd always be an outsider, always alone. All she had to do was breathe in the warm, earthy, and slightly sweet smell of Tomas Gallagher that reminded her of lying in a vineyard beneath the ripening grapes.

One fear remained. A fear worse than never hearing again. A fear that—

Then she became aware of something. It was so foreign that she couldn't make sense of it for a moment. It had been going on for a while.

"Hey!"

She could feel Tomas twist to look at where she lay tucked inside the curve of his arm.

"I can hear the waves on the sand." Whatever her body had done to protect her during the explosion had released its hold on her hearing.

"Really?" Now she would forever know what his voice could sound like—soft, kind, and filled with wonder.

"Really." And then her last fear slid into the night. The fear that she'd never get to hear Tomas Gallagher say, "I love you."

FOR HER DARK EYES ONLY

Kurt fights as a sniper for Delta Force, the most skilled operators in any military. Out on the edge, the line often blurs. This time he sees the edge clearly, and must walk right past it.

Mira has worked as Kurt's spotter in Iraq, Yemen, and a dozen other places. This time they are taking on a "friendly" power, but no question exists—her place lies at his side.

Beyond that line abides a truth that they must learn, a truth fit For Her Dark Eyes Only.

This story was born of many elements.

It was actually the first of the Shooter stories that I wrote. I wanted to plunge deep into how a sniper thinks. That made it one of the few stories written in the first person.

Writing with "I" poses some interesting challenges.

Many writing teachers say that it is terribly restrictive because you can only know what the main character knows. Only walk through their thoughts. No omniscient overview. No other character to see what the other can't... including their own reactions.

But it is also incredibly liberating, because we (both the reader and the writer) get to know exactly what that person is thinking, seeing, and feeling. There grows a very close bond between the reader and the point-of-view character that can't be recreated in the third person by even the most skilled writer.

One of the tricks around that restrictiveness is to alternate chapter by chapter whose first-person point-of-view we experience. I didn't do that. I wanted to go all the way with Kurt. I wanted to see what could drive him, not merely to be a Delta sniper, but to go "off the reservation"—beyond the authorized rules of engagement.

That was my second element.

I'm a pacifist a heart, but there are some people who really *should* be exterminated.

I remember a long discussion on a flight from India to Egypt with a Muslim missionary. This was long before 9/11 and the latest wars of Southwest Asia.

He had been raised strictly in the tradition of Islam and had done no reading outside of his teachings. I've read widely from *The Bible* and the *Book of Mormon* to the teachings of Lao Tzu, Confucius, and Buddha.

Our talk delved deeply into the messages that are common throughout all cultures. The language varies, but there are numerous common threads. For example, in the West we might say, "Do unto others as you'd have them do unto you." In Arabic traditions, "Treat your guest as if it is their home."

My companion pointed out that it is not people of faith who also created the image of "The Koran in one hand and the sword in the other." (Or the KKK's version of "The Bible in one and the lynching rope in the other.") This is done by jihadis, crusaders, or whoever with no respect for the underlying moral laws that are a part of life.

A crime of passion I can almost understand. Sometimes. Rarely.

A crime of pre-meditated death, destruction, or even abuse, I can't understand at all.

I gave that challenge to my Delta warrior, Kurt.

Shortly before writing this story, I was reading of yet another round of Saudi state-sponsored terrorism when I realized that my hands were shaking with fury.

This story is part of how I fight back.

1
————

"Sucks!" I called out to the watch officer as I strode into the command hangar at the ass-end of Riyadh airfield.

Surprising a Delta Force operator with one of my sniper-silent approaches was never a good idea. Doing it to the six-foot-two of officer who stood four inches taller than me and had much broader shoulders was an even worse one.

Part of our low profile stance in Saudi Arabia was that we ran our operation in the shadowy back corner of the most rundown hangar on the base. It was so beat-up that it captured more of the passing sandstorms than it kept out. Delta's watch post was tucked behind a small flock of Night Stalkers' helos and an Air Force four-prop C-130 cargo plane which served as our secure storage and could get us up and out in fifteen minutes if we had to jump in somewhere. At night, with only a single desk lamp on, it was a murky place of shadows and secrets.

"Kurt," was all that Lieutenant Bill Bruce grunted in

reply—about as much as my greeting deserved. Two a.m. shift change, and the country was still cooking so hot that I had probably sweat out a liter just crossing over from the long banks of containerized housing units—CHUs— in the US Spec Ops sector.

My last leave back home on the Oregon Coast was still in my blood and the desert sucked. The six hours that Lieutenant Bruce had just spent on the watch desk also couldn't have been much of lark. So, neither of us had been issued a cheery mood.

"I swear my CHU was shipped over during Desert Storm." The container had two bunks, two chairs, and a toilet in a twenty-foot steel box with an AC unit bolted on one end that groaned, wheezed, and could sometimes drop the inside temperature a whole ten degrees—my home for the last six months that Delta Force had parked my ass here.

"CHUs weren't part of inventory back then, Sergeant." The lieutenant's ex-SEAL was showing through. Those guys never had a decent sense of humor, not even after joining The Unit—what most folks call Delta Force. We were officially CAG, the Combat Applications Group, with a strong emphasis on "Application."

"Maybe you could un-invent them, sir." Then I didn't see any reason to not keep messing with him. "I bet some supply sergeant timewarped it back so that it would corrode and spring sand leaks until I moved in." It was almost plausible. I'd long since learned to never underestimate the power of a quartermaster—especially if you ticked him off.

Still no response.

"I swear, thing's the same age I am and someone should have taken it out to pasture and shot it a long time back." I might have done it myself if we weren't supposed to be keeping such a low profile.

We tried to stay quiet because the Saudis weren't big fans of having US commandos squatting in the heart of their country, no matter how badly they needed us. Being here worked for us too. From Riyadh we were four hundred klicks to Iran, Iraq, Yemen, Syria, and a dozen other disasters waiting to happen. So, during those rare pauses in between assignments, this base was where we squatted and sweat until hot metal and the almost cinnamon tang of blowing dust had become a part of who we were.

The lieutenant kept his blue-eyed gaze flat and his face deadpan.

Thought I'd earned more than that, but there wasn't even a hint of a smile; the bastard was damned hard to read at the best of times. He was married to a seriously cute helo pilot from the Night Stalkers, but I was careful to not even glance at her when Lieutenant Bruce was around. The man might be an officer, but he was also a Unit operator and just as dangerous as any of us. He also hung tight with Colonel Gibson who was more dangerous than all of us combined.

"Anything cooking on the desk?"...*other than the damned desk in this heat?* I grabbed a water bottle out of the kicker fridge and rubbed it across my forehead—so cold it almost gave me a headache. A mission would make the night much more tolerable, but it all looked pretty damn quiet. The folding table supported a stack of silent comm gear, a couple big screens that were supposed to be for situational displays but streamed movies just fine on pizza-and-no beer nights—dry post on Saudi soil.

"Left you some routine crap," Bill flicked a finger against the paper in the in-basket.

"Thanks so much, asshole." I gave it a friendly tone.

He glanced at me. There were certain looks that they only teach in officer's school and this was one of them.

"Thanks so much, asshole Sir." *Shit!* Still nothing. There was no saluting in the field. It might attract a sniper's bullet targeted at whoever that identified as being in charge. But I was tempted just in case there was a sniper on the hunt tonight, because that would at least change the mood.

The lieutenant tapped the pile again, marking it as my top priority, before heading out into the dark heat.

The small fan perched on the edge of the desk helped a little when I dropped into the folding steel chair. Now instead of slowly baking to death, I was going to be put out of my misery much sooner by the blowtorch of fan-driven hot air.

Comms were silent. I logged into the computer and made sure the command message queue was up on the screen. I popped up a second window that showed the regional queue as well. Nothing but a whole lot of quiet. I could have heard a gecko walking on the metal ceiling a dozen meters above me.

Feet on the desk, I pulled over the in-basket and began flipping through it. Some supply chain crap. New sergeant coming over soon. No sign of my reassignment to somewhere, anywhere else, not that I was expecting one anytime soon but I could always hope. I'd give up my next pay for two damned minutes of Oregon Coast air— just a walk with my lady down the long sand beaches; the wind off the Pacific rolling in cool, wet, and so fresh it was like no one had ever breathed it before.

Dreaming of other places, I had the manila folder from deep in the pile half open before I froze in place. The chill up my spine had a whole lot more to do with Arctic training than Saudi desert.

I almost shouted out *Landmine!* to warn everyone around me—except if I did, only the plane and helicopters were there to hear me.

I was sitting alone and holding a viper made out of beige manila—a viper way more dangerous than the flesh-and-blood kind.

"Classified-Secret."

A big red stamp on the cover. Typically illegible authorization signature. An innocuous number on the tab.

Why the hell was a classified document buried in the watch desk in-basket? I wanted to take the damn thing and ram it right up the lieutenant's ass for leaving such a thing out to be found.

Protocol said to lock it up in the secure vault resting under the table, then report it to command and send an armed guard to take the lieutenant into custody. Reality said to lock it up and suggest to his boss that the man get a refresher course in proper handling of classifieds.

Instead, I eased it open.

"Eyes only!"

Viper? Hell. I was holding a damned grenade with no sign of the pin or handle—and three of five seconds gone.

Should have slapped it closed. Should have the fucking lieutenant shot.

Instead I read the damned thing.

2

———

Mira slipped into the hangar. The way that woman moved was like nothing else I'd ever seen. There weren't all that many Spec Ops women, but she made it look natural...natural and dangerous as hell.

We'd quietly shared enough two-week leaves for me to know that both assessments were accurate about her in every way. Dusky skinned enough to pass as a native anywhere in the Middle East, her night ops black hair curled down to her shoulders. Her face was forgettably normal (which was ideal for an operator)—forgettable unless you knew the woman who hid so carefully behind it.

She didn't ask why I called and woke her. Instead, she sat down on another chair and waited.

I turned the folder over in my lap and showed her the front.

A shrug.

I peeled back the front flap enough to reveal the "Eyes Only."

Her gaze shot up and inspected me carefully. I could see her connecting pieces, putting together the question that I wasn't willing to speak aloud. I wasn't asking the question of my lover. I was a sniper asking a question of my spotter.

A sniper has to move undercover in any environment —hard to do as a single man, much easier with a woman at his side. He also needs a spotter to watch his back and cover the wider view while he's busy.

She excelled at both roles.

Whether we were on overwatch protecting door-kicker troops working the street below or out in the weeds, Mira didn't miss a thing. We were one of the top teams operating.

Mira would, of course, integrate all this into her consideration about the question I had asked by flashing the folder. She knew she could stand up and walk away with no hard feelings, but she also knew I wouldn't have called her lightly.

This time I couldn't read what was behind her dark eyes any more than the damn lieutenant's light ones, but she reached out and took the file.

Based on the data in the folder, I began studying city maps and drone overflight images on the dual screens while she read.

3

———

"WE'RE NOT SUPPOSED TO BE HERE, KURT!" ONLY MIRA'S eyes showed through the narrow slit of the *niqab* headpiece she'd worn as we worked our way across Riyadh looking like any other Arab couple.

"Then leave." It came out harsher than I intended, but I was feeling the pressure too. "Sorry." The "home" we were surveying would have been a mansion in Los Angeles, a damned big one. Here it was called a palace but that didn't make it any smaller.

I could tell by the narrowing of her eyes that Mira was scowling at me, which I ignored just as I had been for the other fifty times she'd said it since last night. Though once she'd read the file there hadn't been any question of not going in together.

Something about complaining always made her feel like she was in control whenever the situation was spinning out of control, but I knew that about her and usually let it slide.

Didn't matter anyway.

Once we stepped past this point we'd be in it deep and the only way out was going to be even uglier than the way in. In truth, all bets were on a one-way ticket.

We weren't supposed to be here—no one could know. Literally... No. One. That's what the Unit specialized in, but even by our standards this was beyond dark and creepy.

The objective was inside this monstrosity. Four stories with a double-height first. Delta named the sides of a building from front entrance around clockwise by the alphabet for easy reference—front door wall was "A," next wall to the left "B," and so on. Don't know if this place would have fit in the alphabet. Shining white, two big wings, attached garages that would fit twenty cars, bathhouses between the two pools, a clubhouse by the putting greens... The place was absurd.

Thankfully, that worked in our favor as the target would never think guards were needed every foot. It was old enough that the cameras and sensors had been installed later, making them both easy to spot and fewer than they should have been.

Mira was right though, this was the last check-in, the last point to turn back.

I flicked a "Move Out" sign, but more as a question. At Mira's nod, we shed our outer robes. From here on, blending in wasn't the issue, being invisible was. Dark camouflage, night-vision goggles, and minimal gear other than our weapons and a lot of extra rounds. We headed in.

They didn't train snipers in The Unit to waste time.

Our training was all about achieving results. I wasn't the first operator to have used that as an excuse in marginal conditions and I wasn't about to be the last. Because we delivered, Joint Special Operations Command did a fine job of looking the other way.

When we were rolling up Iraqi terror cells back in the war, the Status of Forces Agreement prohibited US counterterrorism raids without an Iraqi court-issued warrant. To solve this, Spec Ops built courtrooms in every major city in-country and made sure they were manned by US lawyers and a local judge 24-7. Still, the ops in the field sometimes outstripped the speed of the courts. When we had a known terrorist in our sights, the lawyers back-timed the judge's signature and the judge turned a blind eye.

Were mistakes made?

Very few and only very quiet ones.

The Unit wasn't SEAL Team Six. ST6 made noise about their ops—Captain Phillips, bin Laden, Jessica Buchanan; high profile wasn't in our program.

With command's and the Iraqi courts' authorization, four thousand Al-Qaeda leaders were removed in the last four years of the Iraq War. So quietly that local Al-Qaeda required years of inattention by Iraq Security Forces in order to rebuild into any level of viable threat.

Noise wasn't the Unit's way. Wasn't really ST6's either, but the newsies had latched onto them so hard they could barely function—better them than us.

This op wasn't exactly authorized either.

No war existed here.

No warrant had been signed.

No order had been issued.

Except for what was in that goddamn folder, which probably no longer existed. When I hand-delivered the thing back to Lieutenant Bruce, an "Oh, thanks Master Sergeant," was all I got for my trouble.

That and a headful of crap I wished I never knew.

This was a friendly country, an ally, even the kind that The Unit usually cultivated—a dangerous one.

The Kingdom of Saudi Arabia spent more per capita on their military than any other country. Number One. The Big Kahuna. The KSA spent three times the amount that Singapore, Israel, or even the US did. Five times more than anyone in the next tier down. A higher percentage of their annual GDP than anyone except North Korea and that place was fucked anyway.

Mira and I slid in through the garage: Bentley, Rolls, Lambo, Porsche, not a whole lot of American other than a Hummer and a Tesla. No Japanese at all. Got to admit that the Lamborghini Countach was a classic that almost stopped me in my tracks—it was a low-slung thing of beauty.

Mira nudged me with the butt of her rifle. "Boys and toys," she whispered but I could hear the laugh in it.

I hadn't felt much like laughing since I'd spent the hours reading that goddamn document before I called Mira.

The KSA was run by one king and seven thousand princes, all blood relatives. Family reunions must be hell. Especially with how these guys got along. Internecine conflict didn't begin to describe it.

And when huge bulks of oil fortunes were on the move, it got messy.

Defense Ministers took billion dollar bribes from military vendors like it was cotton candy. Lately the Saudis had been going through Ministers of Defense and the Interior so fast it was a wonder anyone was left in the royal family, because sure as shit if you were one of the top thirty, you were related by direct blood to the king and your motives were suspect.

Some of the princes were pro-American, some anti-. That didn't bother me any and it hadn't bothered Mira when I was giving her the lay of the land. It's not like that was any news to us. Both of our fathers had done the Desert Storm dance, staging in The KSA to clear Saddam Hussein out of Kuwait. They'd both brought back plenty of stories and a gutful of hate.

But I hadn't meant to suck Mira all of the way in. I had just wanted her take on the file's contents. Was I reading too much into that "Eyes Only" report or... She didn't think I was.

Saudi Prince Abdul Malik Hassan was demanding heavy "donations" for feeding the US with prime intel. Turned out that he also was taking prime intel on our movements, and selling them back to every bidder.

Twenty-five of my SEAL Team 6 brothers—I only sneer at them to keep them on their toes—were in a Chinook helo that was shot down in Afghanistan in 2011. Deep research pointed to Abdul feeding the intel to Al-Qaeda shooters—no proof.

Again when ST6 had been repulsed by Al-Shabaab terrorists in Somalia, Abdul's call had been traced there as well. He had a whole network of brothers, cousins, and sons servicing the intel in both directions—a clusterfuck that involved a dozen princes and twenty more besides. We needed the intelligence reports he gave us, so the CIA had labeled him "Untouchable."

There were other opinions in that damn file. The Saudi Defense Minister, the US Secretary of State, the Head of the Joint Chiefs... They all agreed that Abdul had walked way too far over the lines in both directions. But no one wanted to do the deed. No one wanted the CIA to find out they'd done the deed.

And neither Mira nor I gave a shit about any of them.

It was the price of what Abdul took...

I no longer had brothers, not outside the service.

No family outside the service.

My brother Stan found heroin, then God, then tried combining the two so that he could go meet God face to face. He never came back to tell me if it worked. Mom had long since walked away and Dad eventually ate his gun. We weren't what you'd call...close.

"Close" is what I found in The Unit, even before I met Mira Stenkowski.

Five years in Special Forces, tromping ass with the 3rd SFG Green Berets, before I could even apply to The Unit. Delta Assessment Phase spent a month proving that nobody loved me—but I already knew that, so it didn't knock me out like so many others. Combined with being tough as hell, I made the five percent cut. And they took me in.

All the way in.

The Unit did that. These weren't fellow soldiers. The

guys weren't some inbred clan like Prince Abdul's. These were men, and now the few women, that I'd stand at the tip of the spear for. Give me the first hit. Take me down first. Because that's the only way you're going to get at me and mine.

But Abdul didn't believe that.

4

———

For three days we watched him.

Mira and I crawled in and watched him. We lived in his house. We smelled the food he ate. We watched him fuck his wives at night from so close we could smell the sex on him afterward. We didn't drink water so that we wouldn't have to pee. We didn't eat so that we wouldn't have to shit.

Mira and I were a US Delta Force sniper team—so invisible that we weren't even there.

But we were and we listened.

Abdul had a rage in him. That part of him I recognized. That part of him I knew down to my bones. Before The Unit, it had twisted inside my guts like a knife every time I thought of my family. I didn't beat or kill, but I knew what drove him.

He got angry at a wife for not being eager to receive him. After he beat her, and used her hard, he stated the fateful "I divorce you" three times—all a guy had to do to end a marriage in this culture. At that moment she lost rights to any of her children and was banished back to her family, never to emerge from the shame again. Mira almost took him down at that point, but I held her back. Abdul wasn't the only reason we were here.

A cousin of his—who had demanded a mere hundred grand for selling the allied bombing patterns over a terrorist-held city when he should have earned half a million—was dismissed, without the grace-saving of "based on his request" in the announcement of his departure. His career, his life in Saudi politics was finished. Mira and I laid a bet that his fortunes would be gone in twenty-four hours and his family in forty-eight. *End it now, Dude.*

And still we waited in thirsty silence.

We were the hum in an air-conditioning vent, a shadow behind a palm tree, a breath on the wind. We sucked on pebbles to draw precious saliva to soothe aching throats.

Three long days we waited and watched. On the long watches I wondered if the goddamn lieutenant had reported us AWOL—away without leave—or if he'd left a simple "on assignment" on our registers. We were past that now. Even the ache didn't matter, only the mission.

The self-assigned mission.

Night four.

Abdul's private war council had finally been called.

Out in the great courtyard of his home, an evening of food and debauchery on a grand scale convened. His war council of thirty of his closest and most trusted— brothers, cousins, sons. All of his sons.

"Go, Mira. Go now. While you can." I was assembling my McMillan TAC-50 sniper rifle.

"That boat sailed the minute we stepped off the reservation, Kurt." She began lining up magazines for me. Five rounds per mag of .50 BMG sniper-grade ammo; four to a pound and as long as the five dollar bill each one cost.

We'd scouted the ideal spot, found it in the bastard's bedroom.

A monstrous bed, satin sheets the size of pool covers, red Persian rugs on white marble floors, gold fixtures in a bathroom big enough to park a couple Humvees in. Wealth dripped out of the faucets and shone from the crystal chandeliers. I'd never seen anything like it and frankly never wanted to again. It was cold in this blazingly hot country. More frigid and heartless than a winter storm blowing in off the north Pacific.

Mira had quietly spoken with the four current wives —apparently none of them were very fond of their husband-prince and the dismissed wife had been a favorite in their circle. For their own safety in deniability afterward, Mira had tied them up in the bathroom. Then we'd barricaded ourselves in.

The only opening was the French doors that swung out into the night. An ornate dresser of inlaid English rosewood turned into a shooting stand placed well inside the room. With the flash suppressor and an extra foot of silencer, I'd attract little attention. Only a perfect shot from the courtyard could find me, though we both expected one eventually would.

Mira's family had been little better than mine. Just

like me, her brothers and now the occasional sister, were in the Spec Ops community. We both knew what was coming for us and, without a word, we were both willing to pay the price if it came to that.

Abdul's war council spread out in the marble-paved courtyard below me—acres of the stuff. Out in the exact center stood a circle of tables covered with pristine white cloths and laden with an unimaginable bounty. Buckets of iced caviar, great slabs of pâté, whole sides of beef that could feed hundreds, all served by lightly clad women who had clearly been paid to not complain no matter what was done to them.

The range was so close that I couldn't miss.

The Canadian TAC-50 was twenty-six pounds and six-feet of the baddest rifle in the business. Two of the three longest sniper shots ever confirmed as kills had flown out of TAC-50 barrels—each over two thousand meters and I didn't have a single shot here over two hundred. I'd selected the beast just in case I had needed the long shot. Instead I had easy targets and massive rounds to punch with.

I dialed back my Schmidt-Bender scope all the way from the thousand-yard zeroing I kept the rifle set for. My bullets were going to drop less than two inches before impact at this range.

We'd all been scrubbed. There was no serial number on either scope or weapon. The only ID Mira and I carried was phony as hell and identified us as mercenaries gone hunting—traceably hired by the remains of a cell of terrorists Abdul had fucked over in

Pakistan. Even if we got out clean, we'd "drop" those IDs somewhere that they'd be discovered.

US intel services wanted him in place. US and Saudi military—and any grunt with even half a brain—wanted him gone no matter what the CIA said.

He was about to be erased.

I was committing an act of war. Killing thirty of the King of Saudi Arabia's immediate relatives couldn't be shrugged off. One or two might be overlooked, but Abdul had built his network too well and just cutting the head off the serpent wouldn't be enough.

Worst case scenario? There would be two dead mercs who would never be identified, except by Combat Applications Group Lieutenant Bruce—who'd known exactly what he was doing when he left that "Eyes Only" report for a sniper and his spotter, both with no families outside The Unit.

I snapped in the first magazine with a gentle click and worked the bolt to load the first round so softly that it wouldn't have disturbed a cricket.

Two hundred meters away, I stared straight into Prince Abdul Malik Hassan's face through my scope. His head filled my view. It was thrown back in a laugh and it would have been so easy to feed the round to him, right down his throat.

You always heard when an ST6 SEAL died in action. His brothers saw to that, but that wasn't our way. When my best friend went down in Yemen, his family never knew how it happened. But I knew, now that I'd read the file—they traced it to Abdul giving away our plans. When my bunkmate lost both arms and his eyesight in the Ukraine, Abdul might as well have pulled the trigger.

"Not yet, Abdul," I whispered down the long length of my sweet rifle.

I shifted my aim.

Not yet.

First you need to watch your family die.

5

───────

THE UNIT DOESN'T BELIEVE IN SUICIDE MISSIONS. DELTA'S mission is to deliver results.

I'd arrived in this place knowing the odds. I care about my life and Mira's, maybe more than anyone because an operator goes in knowing the risks—I take them every day. It would take so little to erase everything except someone's memory of me. A stray round, a single mistake.

Training taught me that, but it might not have been enough. I wanted Abdul so badly that I would have seen it through even if there had been no chance of escape.

It was Mira who had taught me that there was more, so much more. We'd slowly discovered it together, in each other. Two people discovering that there was family beyond our brothers and sisters of war. Until we ultimately found true family in each other. There was nothing we wouldn't do for one another.

Nothing.

We began.

It was messy, but it was fast. After three days lying in wait, it was no more than an eyeblink. One heartbeat between shots and two to reload. Just thirty seconds to clear the courtyard of every target—but one.

Then Abdul went down, hard. He went down screaming in panic and running away from the circle of the dead: his murdering council of friends and relatives. For him I used three full magazines, fifteen rounds, all blasted from the big TAC-50 to take him apart one piece at a time.

Toward the end I was peripherally aware of other gunfire—silenced rounds on a different beat. Mira had my back. Kept me safe. But that wasn't my focus. That's why I had a spotter and if she wasn't good enough, we were both done.

She was. Guards who had streamed in from the sides had died in a broad ring around the courtyard

The silence echoed through the palace, Abdul's final scream no more than a memory in the vast marble plaza. Our gunfire had been quiet pops never heard beyond the French doors. Beside many of the dead lay drawn weapons, but lacking a target, no shot was fired.

Mira and I eased back through the streets of Riyadh in the soft cool breath of the pre-dawn desert. She walked two steps behind me, as a *niqab*-clad woman should follow her man: respectful, hidden. Her rifle, like mine, still warm from use, now lay hidden beneath the long folds of her robe. Only her eyes showed.

But in my mind's eye she moved beside me, her dark

hair floating free in the ocean's winds as we held hands
and walked together down the beach in a soft, cool
Oregon rain—her dark eyes bright with the joy of being
alive.

LOVE'S SECOND CHANCE

Delta Force operator Hector Garcia's mission as scout for the take-down of a Mexican cartel leads him straight into a gun battle.

Hired gun Alejandra Martinez prowls at the heart of it. The woman who told him to leave town five years ago looks and fights even better than back then.

Only together can they hope to find Love's Second Chance.

INTRODUCTION

For this tale, I sought a lighter tone, though the subject matter is no less upsetting than in *For Her Dark Eyes Only*.

The drug wars of Mexico affect far more than the flow of drugs into the US. I've come back to this time and again in my stories, trying to somehow understand it, to somehow see some light in all of the darkness.

Do I blame the addicts in my country and others for creating the demand? Or the big pharma who helped so many become addicted? Do I blame the farmers in Colombia just trying to make a living? The cartels who control them? The transporters, the dealers, the warlords, the corrupt politicians... The list seems unending.

So, I chose to fight my small battles of hope.

For me, this concept goes back to long before I began writing.

I'm not some politician or corporate magnate who has the ability to influence large groups of people. I'm a deep introvert and, while I'm a wielder of words, rhetoric is not my chosen field of battle.

Asking myself how I could make a difference is what led me to tales like this one. Seeking out little glimmers of light and hope which show how much more we can be than who we currently are.

For this story, I wanted to look at another aspect that is even deeper in Delta Force training than shooting—adaptability. Their training includes the ability to assess and react *on the fly* at a level that no one else can achieve. Part of that is accomplished by training so constantly. The only time a Delta Force operator *isn't* training, is when they're in battle.

They are taught to continuously rethink every action and to layer that on top of such a deep skill set, that pivoting from one plan to another becomes honed into an instinctual ability. The fact that they can make that pivot on the fly as a team is simply mind-boggling. It's something that doesn't fit well in a short story, though I did try to capture that essence in the four Delta Force novels.

However, I was certainly able to do that for a one-man operation.

And for motivation?

What better than a second chance at finding true love.

1

—————

"You really stepped in some shit this time, Alejandra Martinez." She didn't even know where to direct her fire. Or if she should fire at all.

Lying prone on the roof of the highest building in the area, a whole two stories, gave her the best vantage of the cesspool that had been her hometown for over twenty-five years. US-Mexican border towns sucked, especially when they were on the Mexican side. But she'd never found a way to leave it.

If she started shooting over the low parapet of aged adobe, they'd know she was up here and that could start to suck really fast. Of course another couple of hours up here in the midday sun baking her butt on an adobe grill and maybe she would be ready to shoot all of the assholes who had conspired to trap her up here. They'd gotten blood on her new jeans and sneakers, which was really pissing her off. At least it wasn't hers.

"Next time you're stuck in a street war and trying to survive, remember to bring milk and cookies. Or at least some water." Good reminder, if she ever got out of this one. A six of cold beer sounded good too.

Life had been so much simpler twenty-four hours ago. She'd had a lover, a lousy-as-shit job—making it only a little better than her lover—and something that sort of resembled a place to be.

Now she had a cartel war surrounding the building she lay on top of, and her job was dead—her former employer had owned most of the blood she was wearing. Too bad her job had been to protect his stupid ass. He'd not only been stupid enough to piss off the Alvarado cartel that controlled all the contraband traffic through this town, he'd neglected to tell her he was also setting up the street gangs for a hard fall. They'd found out. Everyone wanted him dead and it was hard to blame them.

The steady crack of automatic gunfire and the hard thwaps of bullets impacting on stone and metal echoed up and down the streets below. These guys were using ammo like it was free. As far as she could tell they were either fighting over who got to claim taking the idiot down, or they were having a gunfight just for the hell of it.

"This town is really going down the toilet."

"Wasn't all that impressive to begin with," a deep voice resonated from close behind her.

As she swung around, a big hand grabbed the barrel of her rifle, stopping it halfway to its new target.

There'd been no sound.

No warning. Not a creak or shift of the rotten roof timbers.

A big *muchacho* knelt close behind her on the roof. He was loaded for action. He held a combat rifle in one hand and her rifle barrel in the other as calmly as if it was the other end of an umbrella or something. Despite his light jacket she could see a pair of Glock 19s in twin shoulder holsters and would wager he had more ammo and another hidden carry or two on him.

A glance past him—the roof access hatch was still closed and latched.

"How the hell did you—" But then she recognized him and knew. "Hector Garcia? Haven't seen your pretty face since Marina was still a virgin." Which was close enough to never. Her little sister had probably seduced her first boy from side-by-side bassinets at the hospital and hadn't slowed down since. At times it was hard to tell if she was a whore or just a slut.

Actually, Hector's wasn't a pretty face, not even the part that wasn't covered by his wrap-around shades and a scruff of three-day beard that looked good on him. He'd broken his nose twice that she knew of, and now maybe a third time by the look of it. She still remembered the knife fight that had earned him the wavering scar from jawline to temple. His dark hair was long, the way he'd worn it ever since he'd lost an ear during a street brawl. He might be a mess, but Hector also looked really good. He used to be one of those slender and dangerous types. Now he was a powerfully wide and dangerous type.

And at the moment...she must look like shit. *Just perfect.*

She'd been riding *guarda* on a candidate for congress presently bleeding out in the middle of the plaza. What *idiota* campaigned in favor of building a wall on the Mexican side of the border to stop drugs and illegal emigration? That was American-style craziness. But he'd paid her more than she could make anywhere else even marginally legal—which meant he was also on the take in a dozen different ways and worried about it. She could have defended him against one or two shooters. But the two gangs duking it out on the streets below had brought them to his speech by the truckload. She'd dropped four before her sense of self-preservation kicked in.

Now Alejandra was really pissed about the blood on her. She'd also crawled through a shattered luncheon buffet on her way up to the roof. Total mess.

Not usual at all for her to think about how she looked in the middle of a gunfight, but she and Hector had a past —even if it was a long-ago past—and her last shred of vanity had been drowned in reeking mole sauce and blood.

He let go of the barrel and she sat up to get a better look at him.

"Shit, woman!" He placed a big hand on top of her head and shoved her back down onto the roof.

Moments later a single bullet cracked by overhead. She'd drawn exactly the kind of attention she hadn't wanted.

Hector rose quickly onto one knee, then swung his rifle up so fast she could barely follow it. No time to aim. No time for anything. He just fired: two shots, a hesitation with a slight shift upward, then a third. He dropped back down. "That should take care of that."

She'd been a shooter of one form or another ever

since she was little: possum as a kid, armadillos to put meat on the table after Dad had bugged out, and bad guys as a policewoman—until the drug lords made that too dangerous a beat. But she'd never seen anything even close to what Hector had just done. He'd barely even looked for the target. Maybe the sound of the bullet had been enough. Maybe for him. And she knew if she tracked down the corpse—for she had no doubt that's all it was now—it would have two holes close together in the chest and one more in the head.

There was certainly no return shot whistling aloft from below.

"Sorry," she should have stayed down.

"*De nada!* So," Hector lay on the roof beside her. "You busy much?"

"You saw the body in the plaza?"

"Yeah."

"That was my meal ticket. No major loss—wasn't much of a lover either."

Hector's face darkened at her second statement.

She swung the butt of her rifle into his gut, aiming between a pouch of ammo and a Glock 19. She caught him hard enough to earn her an angry grunt.

"You been gone, hombre. You don't get to judge shit."

He shrugged one shoulder in agreement, but didn't look much happier about it.

Well, neither was she. Especially not with Hector Garcia lying just inches away to remind her of how good her best lover ever had been.

The gunfire down on the plaza was dying down.

Probably running out of ammo at the rate they were using it.

"Why? You got any bright ideas on how to keep me busy?"

"More than few," his easy leer said plenty. But she still knew him well enough to know that sex wasn't the only thing he had on his mind.

2

HECTOR HAD REMEMBERED ALEJANDRA ROSA MARTINEZ AS a total knock-out, but that was nothing compared to what he'd found up on the roof.

He'd come back to his shithole of a hometown for a mission, not looking for her. Not really. In five years his life had totally changed—no reason to assume that hers had stayed the same. Or that she'd be real interested in seeing him. But a few questions about her had led him to the plaza, just as all hell had broken loose.

He hadn't expected to walk into a gunfight, though four years in the US Rangers and another year as a Delta Force operator had let him see the patterns quickly. There was an obvious hole in the battle running from door to door.

The *policia* were wisely hanging back a couple blocks and waiting it out—though they needed a real lesson about how bullets skipped along concrete walls and he hoped they didn't catch one. It was the reason that war zone photos always showed the US military walking up the center of a street rather than hugging the buildings.

But whatever sides were fighting around the plaza and up on the low roofs, the lack of action from the best vantage point spoke volumes. Somebody held the high ground, which meant they were defending it, but there was no sign they were using it. Someone smart—maybe like Alejandra. He got up to the second story inside the building, leaving only a few broken bones behind him. Not a one of them understood that it would hurt less if they'd just let go of their gun when he was ripping it out of their hands.

At a rear, second-story window, he'd managed to reach up high enough to loop his rifle's sling over a protruding outside timber and used his rifle as a ladder to haul himself onto the roof. There he'd been confronted by one of the finest asses he'd ever seen.

How Alejandra had gotten even better looking in the years he'd been gone, he'd never know. It shouldn't be possible, but it was true.

"You done here?" he nodded toward the plaza.

"Shit, you think?" her sarcastic tongue hadn't changed one bit.

"Good. Got a job I could use some help on."

"You show up out of the blue after five years and you suddenly need help from me? Hector, you're an asshole. You know that, right?"

"Sure."

She snarled at him.

"Never argue with a lady when she's right," he threw one of her favorite sayings back in her face.

Her growl went deep and feline, but when he belly-crawled to the roof access, she followed.

He unsnapped the latch without making a sound. She had her rifle ready to aim down when he opened the hatch. With a shake of his head, he warned her off.

He flipped the release and threw the hatch wide.

They both rolled away from it. Moments later, a half dozen wild shots cut upward through the hatch. One shooter. Off center to the right.

He aimed through the roof itself and laid down a short line of fire. Crawling across it earlier, it was clear that it wasn't much of a roof. The rounds punched through easily.

Alejandra did the same from the other side and her angle looked good.

Hector rolled back and dove through.

The shooter was down.

Alejandra dropped in beside him, so close it was hard not to just grab her. With a toe of her boot, she kicked the shooter over. He'd been hit both front and back. She'd always been good, but somewhere along the way, she'd gotten even better.

"Alvarado's eldest. They were both really pissed when I wouldn't marry him. His dad, Miguel, is *not* going to be happy about this." She nudged a boot against him again, hard to believe he was finally dead.

"Good," Hector offered her a smile. "You can tell Miguel yourself when he finds you in his bed tonight."

"That's part of your plan for...whatever?"

It wasn't, but he'd forgotten how much fun it was to

tease her. For a second he thought she might try aiming her rifle at him again and he was ready for that.

Instead she kicked him in the shins. Hard.

3

———

Whatever Hector was into, Alejandra wasn't interested.

But she was.

They scrounged lunch in the deserted first floor café while the gun battle finished dying off around them. They sat side by side in the cool darkness of the kitchen, their backs against the steel door of the walk-in refrigerator and good visibility of both approaches—each with their rifle across their lap. They'd found cold beer, but Hector had opted for water so she'd done the same.

"Where the hell did you go, Hector?"

"North." The only thing north was the US.

"Why?"

His frown said he didn't like that question. Not a bit.

She finished her empanada then nudged his ribs with the butt of her rifle.

"You told me to go. Said you'd kill me if you ever saw me again," his face said that his second empanada tasted like bitter sand. He chucked it under the sink.

Alejandra thought back to the day he'd gone. She'd been furious with him for something, then he'd bugged out and she never had a chance to take it back. What was...

Marina! Her slut of a sister had bragged about taking down Hector.

"You weren't supposed fuck my sister while you were with me."

"Didn't."

She opened her mouth, then shut it again. One thing about Hector, he never lied. He might keep his trap shut, but he never lied.

"Pissed her off some that I wouldn't."

Whereas her little sister lied about everything—and Alejandra always fell for it. Big sisters were supposed to trust their little sisters. But she'd described certain things about Hector that only a lover would know...or someone who'd spied on him making love. "Shit! I'm gonna strangle the little bitch."

Again Hector's indifferent shrug.

"So I tell you to go and you just do? No argument?"

"You had a .357 revolver aimed at my crotch. I'm not gonna argue with that. I know how good a shot you are."

"And you don't even try to come back?"

Hector looked over at her with those sad, puppy-dog eyes of his. She'd never been able to resist those. Six foot of tough hombre was not supposed to have window-to-his-soul kind of eyes, but he always had. "Without you, I had nothing here."

And he hadn't. His family made hers look like all the good bits of a Thalía telenovela.

"Five years." Somehow they'd lost five years. "Five goddamn years."

4

———

Hector leaned his head back against the refrigerator door and closed his eyes. Yeah, he'd abandoned her to this hell for five years. If she'd done it to him, he'd never forgive her. Shit.

Closing his eyes didn't help.

Now he wasn't seeing her long flow of softly curling black hair with just a hint of her grandmother's dark gold, framing that perfect face. He couldn't see the proud curves above her slender waist that he had so loved to bury his face in. But he could smell her: rich, dark, spicy —overlaid with drying mole sauce on her tight jeans. Like a mix of the lush bounty of the goddess Mayahuel and the fierce and deadly earth goddess Tlaltecuhtli. She had seemed that way ever since they'd sat side by side in *primaria* school desks and learned about the ancient Aztecs.

And she was still that even now, squatting in a darkened kitchen waiting out the stupid shit going on outside: lush, dangerous, and so goddamn good to look at.

He'd landed his fair share of bar babes over the years. His ugly excuse for a face drew in as many as it put off. Not a one had been worth even half of Alejandra Rosa Martinez.

He shouldn't have tracked her down; it was just messing with his head. She wasn't essential to the mission—though it was a better angle than the one he'd thought up while planning back at Fort Bragg. His assignment was to investigate and assess, then call for what assets he needed. If he shifted his plan to include Alejandra, he had all he needed right here.

Reading the profile on cartel boss Miguel Alvarado had brought up too many memories, too much anger. He shouldn't have taken the assignment.

Missions can never be personal. The commanders of Delta Force had beat that into his head again and again. Yet this time it was. His hometown. His family that had been destroyed. And now, in a file handed to him like a random draw, he knew why.

But he *had* tracked her down.

He thumped his head back against the refrigerator door.

Just walk away, Hector. You did it to her before, you can do it again. It's safer that way. Better for her. Sucks totally for you. But since when was that anything new?

Even knowing the right course of action, Hector knew he didn't have the strength to do it again. She was all the past he had. There was no way she could fit into his current life—she wasn't exactly the patient housewife sort—but there was no way he could stand to pry her back out of his heart now that he'd found her. Not that he'd ever been able to.

"So, what's Alvarado up to this time—other than gunning down my meal ticket? And why you?" Even her voice—he'd even missed the sound of her voice. He remembered it like yesterday.

Hector sighed. There was no way to resist having her by his side, so he should just give in. Even if it would only be on a mission.

"Miguel Alvarado is known for moving drugs and immigrants across the border. Pain in the ass, but the US has had plenty of bigger fish to fry."

He could feel her shrug as a movement through the cool metal against his back.

"He's gone a whole lot lower—human trafficking for the sex trade—and it's time to shut his ass down."

"Shit!" Her sound of utter disgust said that was news to her. "Why *you*?"

That was actually a hell of a good question. What he'd seen in the file back at Fort Bragg, intel and his commanders had certainly seen as well. His hometown—giving him the best knowledge on the ground. His family—he'd told the stories to the psychologists during induction testing into Delta. That had to be in his files. It didn't take a genius to connect Alvarado and his own family. His family had worked as Miguel's guns until they were picked off one by one. He'd probably have been in the family trade and dead by now too, if not for Alejandra threatening to shoot his balls off. Just him left now.

There was only one thing he'd never told the psychs about, one piece that had remained for him alone.

He opened his eyes and looked at her.

"Because, I'm the best bastard for the job."

5

———

The best bastard she'd ever known.

And now he was going to be a *dead* bastard if she ever got her hands back on him.

Tonight's plan had sounded so simple as they'd hashed it out. No unconsidered twists and turns. Whatever training Hector had gotten in the US, Alejandra saw it shine out of him. He brought up scenarios and variables like it was fact, not guesswork. His easy confidence had made it comfortable to believe and trust him despite his five-year absence.

She tugged against the heavy ropes tied around her wrists, but all it did was abrade her already sore wrists. His plan had been great—right up to the moment she'd stepped off plan and everything had gone to hell.

"I was *not* supposed to end up in Miguel Alvarado's bed, Hector. That was supposed to be a goddamn joke." But she had. The bedroom in Alvarado's hacienda was lush. Dark wallpaper, leather and mahogany furniture, a massive California king bed with satin sheets...and a tie-down ring at each corner.

She still had her clothes on, but it was a good bet that wasn't going to last.

Hector had been careful not to say anything about his life in America, but she'd listened to what he hadn't said. No mention of wife or kids. No mention of anything except "work". That's all he called it: work. Not like it took magic powers to figure out what that meant.

The US didn't send Border Patrol hombres south of the line. They were tough bastards, but they were strictly by-the-book types. The US military didn't invade friendly countries. He'd shrugged off Miguel Alvarado's drug trafficking the way no DEA agent would and she suspected that if Hector was CIA, he'd feel creepier.

He didn't. Hector cut a solid, steady hole in the world gone to shit.

US Special Operations Forces. Green Beret, Ranger... one of those types. Except they'd sent him in on his own. A true specialist. Now she knew how he shot the way he had. Delta Force. No one else operated alone, could do what he did, and made it look so goddamn easy.

He hadn't just gotten out...he'd gotten *way* out and done good besides.

Alejandra fought back the burning in her eyes. For some brief fantasy moment, she'd thought there might suddenly be a way out for her as well.

She tugged at the rope, knowing it was futile.

Today had also offered a lousy as shit lesson about revenge.

Hector had gone for some supplies he'd stashed out

of town—and she'd gone for Marina. If she'd laid low, like he'd said, she wouldn't be here.

Instead, slamming open her sister's door without knocking, Alejandra had found her with a man, of course. Except this one had Marina gagged and was holding a gun on her. The wide terror of her sister's eyes had made Alejandra hesitate for the wrong second.

Someone grabbed her from behind, and before she could fight him off, Marina's captor had simply cocked the hammer of his pistol and put the barrel against Marina's temple. Then he'd smiled at Alejandra.

Hector had told her what Miguel Alvarado was now into, cross-border human trafficking for the sex trade. She wasn't a damn bit pleased that she and her sister were getting to see that first hand.

The two of them had been herded into an underground holding area with two dozen others. By the light of the lone dim bulb, Alejandra could see enough of their coloring and features to tell that most were Guatemalan or Oaxacan—at least half were underage. Refugees no one would ever miss except for the families back home waiting for news that would never come. In the stuffy, crowded cell, Marina had told her that the man who had captured them had been a pissed off ex-lover, one of Alvarado's men, who she'd dumped for being too rough.

They were the only locals waiting to be shipped off.

"My timing seriously sucks," Alejandra looked once more at her reflection in the mirrored ceiling above the bed. Miguel Alvarado was a kinky bastard.

He'd come to survey his "cargo" earlier. He'd merely

grunted when he spotted Marina. But when he'd seen Alejandra, his smile had gone evil. That was how she'd ended up tied to his bed.

So much for hope.

Now it was just a question of how awful the ending was going to be.

Any time in the last five years, death wasn't that unexpected. She'd known her life expectancy in Mexico stank.

But for one brief afternoon, there'd been hope. The loss of that was now doubly devastating.

6

IT HAD TAKEN HECTOR SIX HOURS THROUGH THE sweltering afternoon and until well past sunset to track Alejandra. He'd lost ten years off his life when someone had finally dared to tell him that she and her sister had been taken away—bound. That had cost him half the time, finding that first step.

No other Delta Force assets in the area, nor any that could be in place fast enough.

He got on the radio with the intel boys, but this wasn't America—security cameras didn't hover above every street corner. However, they had been tracking a pending shipment of women. The challenge was not only to rescue the shipment, but to nail Miguel Alvarado red-handed.

Hector's plan had been to screw up the night's logistics badly enough to force Miguel to take a personal and very visible hand. He was too well connected to turn him over to the Mexican authorities, but once across the border, there were other ways to deal with him. They needed him alive, at least long enough to reveal his whole network.

But now Alejandra was gone and the paths had all led here—the massive hacienda several miles out of town. He'd dumped his beater vehicle in a handy arroyo and run the last few miles overland. The adobe wall around the massive compound was topped with glass shard and razor wire. Miguel had always been a rich bastard, but clearly he'd reached new depths that he'd needed to turn his home into a fortress.

Hector slid into the compound, only having to leave two guards down for the count. No dogs, which was a mistake, though there were ways of dealing with them. Just made his job easier. Miguel used to keep pit bulls, until they'd mauled one of his sons.

Hard floodlights blinded guards and cast hard shadows.

The security cameras within Miguel's compound weren't well placed—there were plenty of blank spots where they could be avoided. But they acted as excellent signposts guiding him on which way to go—the more cameras, the more important the area was to Miguel.

Inside the garage, Hector found a trio of hot sports cars (all red)—including a Ferrari that looked like it would be an awesome ride. Further in were a half dozen heavy pickups and SUVs appropriate for transporting a personal militia, and a battered American school bus.

Even as he watched, he saw a line of women and children being led up to it from some underground cellar, but not onto it. Instead, hatches in the yellow sides were opened up and the women were made to crawl inside.

Everyone knew that school buses weren't set up to carry luggage underneath like a Greyhound. To any but the most careful inspection, it would appear empty except for the driver who was bound to have some "legitimate" excuse for crossing the border.

They loaded the right side first. Just before she crawled into the rearmost compartment, he recognized Marina Martinez. The years had been far less kind to her than they had to her sister. There was still a beauty there, but now it looked hard and strained. She also looked terrified. He didn't recognize anyone else.

When the guards finished and moved around to load the other side, he slipped up and unlocked the rear hatch.

"Where's Alejandra?"

"Hector?"

He clasped a hand over her mouth to silence her, then repeated his question.

"Miguel took her," she whispered carefully. "You have to save us. You must—"

"Shh. Too many guards here. I'll come for you later." Before she could protest, he lowered the hatch and relocked it.

And there wasn't time to stop the shipment—he had another priority now.

A quick drop-and-roll beneath a black Chevy Suburban was all that saved him from discovery.

He had the beginnings of an idea and began putting it in place as he slipped deeper into the shadows.

7

MIGUEL SEEMED DISAPPOINTED THAT SHE WOULDN'T scream. His hard slaps only served to piss her off and make her jaw hurt. Fine, as long as he didn't break it—so that she could chew off his face if she got the chance.

He made all sorts of threats and boasts—most having to do with fucking her to death just to teach her a lesson. Apparently rejecting his now-dead son, as well as his job offer to be a shooter for Miguel's illegal operations had really pissed him off. It was hard to tell which had made him angrier.

Too smart to risk freeing her hands or ankles, Miguel used a steak knife to slice away her clothes.

"First me. Then the knife," he wielded it down near her waist. "Don't worry, Alejandra. It will be fast. I have other business to see to tonight as well."

He stripped and knelt above her. Alejandra braced herself for the worst. She wasn't going to cry or beg, not for Miguel's benefit. There had to be more horrid ways to die, she just couldn't think of what they were. She wouldn't cry for him, but inside, where her heart ached, she would cry for what she and Hector might have had.

She closed her eyes as his hot breath landed between her breasts.

"First, I'm going to—" then he squeaked.

Alejandra opened her eyes and couldn't make sense of what she was seeing.

Miguel's eyes were wide with shock.

In the mirror above the bed, she had a bird's eye view of the baddest, angriest warrior she'd ever seen.

She'd thought Hector had looked heavily armed and badass this afternoon. Now he was something else. A pair of night-vision goggles had been pulled up onto his forehead. He wore a vest that hung with two pistols, dozens of magazines of ammo for both pistols and rifles, as well as grenades and flashbangs. His puppy-dog eyes now belonged to a full-grown Doberman—a really pissed one.

And she couldn't see his rifle, not all of it anyway. The muzzle appeared to be jammed well into Miguel's ass. The angle was such that if Hector fired, the round would miss her, traveling up through Miguel's body and out the top of his head. She might get splattered with his brains.

She was fine with that.

"Lose the knife."

She thought she knew all the moods of Hector Garcia, but she'd never seen him so angry, so focused in her entire life.

Apparently, neither had Miguel. The blade clattered to the floor.

"Sideways, slowly, until you're lying facedown on the

bed. You so much as brush against Alejandra and you're a dead man."

Miguel edged carefully away. The rifle moved with him.

"You okay, Alej?"

Ah-lay. A name she hadn't heard in far too long. She couldn't say all of the things that welled up inside her, didn't dare let them out in the world yet. Digging deep, she found something else. "Could do without the goddamn ropes."

Keeping his rifle shoved someplace dark and nasty, he pulled out a big military knife and slashed her bonds.

Her clothes were in tatters. She went and found some others stashed in a dresser: women's, a wide variety, some close enough to her size. *Bastard.*

She came back and picked up the knife Miguel had dropped to the floor and shifted around until he could see her holding it close by his nose.

"How would you like to fuck a knife, Miguel? Be glad to hold it for you. I'll put you down just like I did your rabid dog of a son."

"I need information first," Hector had to slow her down. Not that he could blame her. He felt the same way.

To find Alejandra after all these years and then to come so close to losing her again made him sick. What Miguel had planned for her...the fury rose in a wave that threatened to choke him.

But the 75th Rangers had taught him how to rechannel fury, saving it to focus on the battle moment. Then Delta had taught him how to turn hot fury into cold, until it was a finely-honed weapon.

It didn't take long to get Miguel to spill everything: hierarchy, contacts, combinations to safes, and passwords to his computer. He'd tossed Alejandra a recorder and she'd held it close to his mouth to make sure they didn't miss a thing. How she didn't rip his face off in the process was one of the most impressive displays of restraint he'd ever seen.

Before he let Miguel get dressed, he yanked his rifle

free, and shoved a small breaching charge for blowing open locked doors up the guy's ass.

"See this?" he held the remote up close for Miguel to see. "One press of the button and you explode from the inside out. We clear?"

Miguel nodded hurriedly.

Hector tossed the control to Alejandra who caught it one-handed, then looked at him thoughtfully but didn't say anything.

On their way back to the garage, the three of them walked as if everything was okay, Miguel imperiously waving guards aside. They made a few stops along the way. A small knapsack was soon filled with the contents of Miguel's safe, though Hector didn't bother with the cash. Instead he left an incendiary for whoever opened it next. They picked up Miguel's laptop and smartphone along the way, dropping them into foil bags to avoid anyone tracking them.

In the garage, the bus and most of the SUVs were gone.

"Tell me you have a plan, Hector," Alejandra had picked up several weapons along the way until she was almost as heavily armed as he was. It looked damned good on her. "My sister's out there somewhere."

Hector loaded Miguel and his files into the trunk of the Ferrari—thankfully he wasn't a big man. Then Hector hit him with enough morphine from his Delta med kit to keep a horse down for a day.

He and Alejandra slid down into the soft, black leather of the bucket seats.

Yes, he had a plan. But he had a mission to finish first.

9

From the start, Alejandra decided that she was really glad that she was on the same side as Hector. He definitely put the bad in badass. And then he kept getting better.

In the Ferrari—which was one of the coolest rides she'd ever had (it grabbed low and yanked her ahead like a sexual shot)—they'd caught up to the bus and the escorting SUVs close to the border station.

Hector had simply waved a hand out the window as they passed, for the SUVs to keep following the bus. He'd slipped in ahead of them all just at the border.

Whatever ID he showed the border guard had certainly gotten his attention. After a few whispered instructions, the guard let the Ferrari and the school bus roll through.

Hector stopped the car before the bus was fully out of the border crossing control lane, trapping it there.

The SUVs had hung back at the last moment,

truckloads of armed guards didn't just roll through border crossings.

Hector pulled out a remote control just like the one he'd tossed to her earlier. He had trusted her—trusted her to not kill Miguel unless they needed to, and to do it in an instant if it became necessary. He'd been right on both counts. No one had ever known her as well as he did.

"I didn't want to risk getting them mixed up," then he flipped up the cover on the activation switch of the one he held, offered her an evil grin, and pressed down on it with his thumb.

The three SUVs still on the other side of the border thumped hard, brilliant light shining out all of their windows. Remote control flashbangs.

In moments, the Mexican border patrol, rifles raised, had everyone out of the vehicles and lying on the asphalt, along with a big enough stack of weapons to make sure they spent a long time in prison.

The next moment, their own vehicle and the bus were surrounded by the US Border Patrol.

INS agents gathered up all of the women and children. A very small team in an unmarked black SUV emptied the still-unconscious Miguel and his files out of the Ferrari's trunk. Their eyes had gone a little wide when she handed over the remote trigger on the breaching charge, and told them exactly where it could be found. Then they were gone.

She and Hector turned to watch as the INS began reassuring the frightened women and children. One was handing out blankets, another with water bottles, and even a few stuffed animals for the youngest to cling to.

"Should I give your sister a contact number? Though I'm not sure if someone that sexy should be allowed into the US."

"You *are* a bastard, Hector. I'm the one you're supposed to be calling sexy." But it was hard to put any real heat behind it with the way he was smiling down at her.

Then she thought about it.

Hector was offering to give a contact number to Marina. It would be *his* contact number, to call if Marina wanted to reach *Alejandra*. That meant that whatever happened next, she herself would be with Hector. Discovering that the tiny shred of hope that had nearly died during the evening wasn't so tiny after all just blew her away. That was way better than being called sexy.

"Sure," Alejandra managed after a deep breath to make sure her voice was steady. "She is my sister after all."

He pulled out a slip of paper, wrote his name and a phone number on it and then handed it to her. At his nod, Alejandra stepped into the crowd of women being corralled onto the bus by the INS agents, this time into the seats rather than the hidden compartments.

She couldn't think of anything to say. Some fit of Marina-jealousy had cost her five years of being with Hector. But it would have been five years in the hell that was a Mexican town on the wrong side of the border. Now she was on the north side of the border next to a top

US military soldier. It wasn't up to her to understand how this screwed-up world worked, but she would absolutely make the best of it.

Alejandra handed the slip of paper to her sister. Marina might be a sex-crazed maniac, but she immediately understood what it meant for both of them.

Marina's "Sorry" was the only word that passed between them as they hugged, but it was a long hug and her little sister's smile wished her joy.

Alejandra waited until they were loaded and gone, waving as the bus disappeared into the night.

She turned and saw Hector leaning against the hood of the Ferrari, his big arms crossed over his chest. He'd shed his weapons into the trunk. The black t-shirt that had been under his vest showed just how wonderful his chest had become over the years.

Alejandra stepped up until she was standing between his wide-braced feet.

"What's next?"

"East or west? Your choice, Alej." His deep voice was as soft as the darkness.

"What's waiting for us?" He didn't flinch at the *us*. Instead he unfolded his arms and slipped his hands onto her waist. It was the first time they'd touched in five years and it felt as if they'd never been apart.

"To the east about a day's drive is Fort Bragg, North Carolina. If you're interested, my unit is starting a testing course for new inductees in a couple days. I already called in and got you clearance while you and your sister were talking. I swore up and down that you're a shoo-in.

Which is a safe bet because you are. The test is brutal, but I got no doubts."

Alejandra leaned up against him and his arms came up around her. It was the best place she'd ever been.

"And to the west?" she could barely speak past how tightly he was holding her.

"About a ten-hour drive out of our way is Las Vegas. They've got these twenty-four hour wedding chapels. Again, if you're interested." She couldn't see his smile because she had her nose buried against his chest, but she could hear it.

Once more that surge of everything she wanted to say to him shot through her. She dug down and sought for something that would keep his ego in line. That would let him know that she wasn't that easy. That he couldn't just sweep back into her life after five years and change everything in a day.

Except he already had. A job, the best lover, a team to belong to. A home. He *had* changed things; he'd made a dream she hadn't even known about come true.

"One question."

"Uh-huh?"

She looked up into his beautiful eyes, knowing now it was something she'd get to do for the rest of her life.

"Ten-hour drive?"

"Uh-huh," he sounded pretty damned pleased with himself at her response pointing them west.

"But isn't that in, like, a normal car? That *is* a Ferrari you're leaning against."

This time he smiled along with his grunt of satisfaction.

She didn't bother answering yes before she pulled his face down and kissed him.

Their love was so big that it didn't need to be said.

WHAT THE HEART
HOLDS SAFE

---

*The round that took out the man behind **Delta Force sniper D.K. "Deek" Davies** missed him by inches. The problem? The man behind him had once been a friend—a friend with an inspiring sister who changed his future.*

***Cindy Borman's** lifetime practice of shutting away her heart means nothing when faced with the one man who knows her past.*

Only together can they face What the Heart Holds Safe.

I love second-chance tales almost as much as I enjoy the themes of triumph and true love. This is definitely another one of those.

One of the things I loved about this story was Delta Force's reputation as the "silent warriors."

It runs deep.

There's a saying among Delta of something to the effect, "If you didn't want anyone to know, why did you send a SEAL?"

Delta operators are notorious for how little they say. I've heard regular Army helicopter pilots refer to, "Oh yeah, we occasionally carried a load of those guys who don't talk. No insignia, but that told us they were Delta."

All of the tell-all books that are published by former SEALs just make Delta operators laugh. They may respect them as warriors—after all, SEAL Team 6 (DEVGRU) training is probably just as deep—but as blabbermouths? SEALs just piss off a Delta operator.

I wanted to explore that silence. Where does it come

from? Why do they hang onto it? *And...*what happens if they fall for a woman who is just as tight-lipped for reasons of her own?

The rooftop setting of the opening has two details from the books and action reports that I read after seeing *13 Hours: The Secret Soldiers of Benghazi* and *American Sniper*—the surreal ornamentation of Libya's rooftops and the helmet trick, respectively. The rest of it is all me.

I spent thirty years working as a project manager in seven different industries, ultimately volunteering as a certification trainer as well. And one thing that's drilled into our heads is that ninety percent of a project manager's job is making sure that communication occurs.

So, I set a hero and heroine who have no skills for communicating outside of battle. I saddled them with no ability to talk about feelings—until the very ending.

Then I sat back and watched the story unfold.

1

____

THE ROUND THAT TOOK OUT THE US ARMY RANGER behind D.K. "Deek" Davies passed less than six inches from his ear. Not worth even noting except for the harsh supersonic *snap* as the bullet rushed by. Then the Ranger collapsed against him which screwed up his next shot, sending it high and to the right. Guy shouldn't have been hovering so close that he collapsed forward when hit.

Deek shrugged, the Ranger slid off his shoulder and collapsed to the ground.

"Shit!"

It was Jimmy Borman. His eye was gone, blood dripping through the squeezed-tight eyelid, the other eye staring wide. A straight-in brain shot. Going home in a box.

"Shit!"

Jimmy had no more home that he did. Certainly not one to go back to.

Deek forced his breath to steady and put his eye back to the sniper scope.

"Shit!" Not Jimmy. Please. It couldn't—

Deek had a shooter out there that he had to stay focused on so he didn't allow himself to look down and confirm what he'd already seen. All he knew was that this goddamn Libyan sniper was going to go down and go down hard.

The question was, where had he gone?

The target couldn't be dumb enough to stay in the same spot as his last shot, but Deek had to check anyway. Nope. Now he'd have to wait for their sniper to try for someone else before...

"Brand, get up here."

While he was waiting for his fellow Delta Force operator to belly crawl across the roof from where he lay with the rest of the Ranger protection squad, he did look down. And cursed himself for doing so. He'd been thrilled to see Jimmy after eight years—the closest Deek ever had to a childhood friend. Embedded one fucking month and...this. Deek reached over and flipped open Borman's heart pocket—the left breast pocket of his inner vest. (For now he'd just think of him as Borman. Keep the wall up, at least until this was done.) No letter, just the slick feel of a photo. Deek tugged it out to see who he'd left behind. Guy was real close-mouthed about whether or not he had a girl.

Deek had meant for it to be just a quick peek, praying there wouldn't be a photo with kids. There wasn't. It was Jimmy's sister Cindy—so stunningly blond and happy. Oh Christ! If there was ever a woman he didn't want to see again it was her. No such luck. It would be up to him to make The Call. Then the obligatory visit next time he was stateside. Some decent act—and that was a whole lot of suck. So much for keeping the fucking wall up.

Brand crawled up beside Borman, three more Rangers were hunkered down covering his six (making sure no one snuck up behind him while he was focusing on bagging the sniper out there). Brand started to roll Jimmy over.

"Too late for him." Deek tucked Cindy's photo into his own pocket and ignored Brand's watchful gaze. He and Jimmy went way back, as far as Deek ever cared to remember, but there was no time to feel now. That was for later. Focus.

"Get his helmet and his rifle. Pop it up over that." He nodded at a stretch of stone banister along the far end of the rooftop. "Duck and weave. Make it look quick but not too smart."

When the helmet came free they both looked away to avoid seeing the bloody mess their friend had become. Borman had been tasked as Deek's close-quarters protection while Deek was doing his countersniper gig and concentrating farther afield. Deek had been looking forward to recommending him for the next Delta testing cycle because the kid had made himself just that damn good. Not so much now.

Deek went back to the scope of his TAC-50 rifle and watched. A slow sweep of the general area. Still no movement. If he were an ISIS shooter— No! Don't stereotype. If his opponent was a smart sniper instead of some dumb kid with a gun, the shooter would be headed...west. Get under the setting sun to blind Deek. It might work, if the sun were half an hour lower, but it wasn't.

Valuing his fingers, Brand had jammed a knife into the bloody padding at the back of Borman's helmet. He eased the helmet up, until barely visible over the wall, then pulled it back down.

Deek shifted his attention west. Maybe behind the tall planter...or the elephant statue. Libya was thick with ornate rooftop ornamentation, much of it riddled with bullet holes from Gaddafi's fall and the disaster that had wracked the country ever since. Rooftop gardens, once the private sanctuaries of the rich and powerful, were now shredded sniper havens.

In his peripheral vision he could see Brand shifting Borman's helmet sideways instead of ducking back down before moving. Then he eased the barrel of Borman's M4 rifle up over the wall.

The sniper's muzzle flash was less than two meters from where Deek had finally centered his scope. He shifted right, compensated an extra half mil mark for the afternoon breeze. Nine hundred meters. His sniper scope was zeroed at a thousand, close enough. In less than half a second, he had the first of three planned shots winging toward the sniper: round one if he stayed put...

Deek heard the *crack* of the sniper's bullet passing by him—farther away this time—as he unleashed his second round.

Round two if the sniper stood up from his shot...

The incoming missed the decoy helmet and splatted on the wall of the building behind them, now just another new divot in the concrete. *Get sloppy when you rush, Mr. Shooter.* Also not smart enough to send two bullets.

Deek stayed steady, waited an extra heartbeat, and fired the last one.

...and round three if the sniper continued moving to the west.

The sniper rose to a low crouch, Deek's first shot—after point-four seconds of travel time—caught him in the abdomen. The second in the jaw. And he must have been tensed to jump to the west, because he managed a single stumbling step forward. His spotter rose to steady him and instead caught the slightly delayed third shot in the head—the two of them collapsed out of sight. The TAC-50's half-inch rounds delivered enough energy, even at nine hundred meters, that neither of them were getting up ever again. Just like Borman.

He and Brand waited fifteen minutes, but no one else took the helmet bait that they tried twice more. The sniper had been potshotting the Parliamentary Building all day yesterday, taking out two representatives and a guard, as if the new government didn't have enough problems in this clusterfuck of a country. Now at least *this* bastard was done with that shit, forever.

Between them they carried Borman (Borman, not Jimmy, getting that wall back up) down the three flights, letting the Rangers take the lead. Normally the Rangers would carry their own and Deek would have let them. But even if they hadn't seen each other in eight years, this was Jimmy Borman and they had a history. He'd been there for Jimmy when he was a screwed up teen, and he was here for him now. Deek sat beside him when they piled into the pair of battered Kia Cerato sedans that had brought them here.

They hauled Jimmy into the safe house and slid him into a body bag. No embedded reporters here, so at least his death would have that much peace. He'd go down as a "training accident" in some other theater, because it was a public "fact" that Delta was not currently operating in Libya.

Now, finally, Deek could let himself feel. Could take time to remember. He'd liked Jimmy, ever since he was the obnoxious kid down the block always tagging after his big sister. He'd had "feisty little shit" down cold then. Eight years later, when he showed up as six-one of badass Army Ranger, he still had it down cold.

Somewhere along the way, he'd taken to tagging after Deek, two lost loners in teenage hell. And again this last month when their units joined up for a little housecleaning in one of the worst countries on the globe. Jimmy had eaten up everything Deek could tell him about Delta. He'd gone from scrawny shit to one tough dude; he said it came from following in Deek's tracks, which was kind of cool.

They'd taken to exchanging hard punches and shouting, "Kick-ass bros!" whenever they headed out on a mission. Damn! Never again.

They slid Jimmy into the cool cellar until they could move him out under cover of darkness. When had little shit Jimmy Borman gotten so damn heavy?

And why did the one thin photograph in his pocket weigh ten times more?

2

———

Cindy felt the man standing at the door to her office before she saw him. She instantly hit a hotkey to secure the military data and lock her screen before she turned. And then wished she hadn't looked—wished she wasn't in Africa at all.

Sergeant Derek Kyle Davies stood exactly on the threshold of her doorway, looking just as upset to be here as she was to have him here. The eight years since she'd last seen him had barely changed him at all. He was a little broader of shoulder and a little darker of expression, but she'd know him anywhere. She suspected that his years in Delta Force had done nothing to improve his limited range of expressive grunts.

Perfect.

That meant it was up to her. As usual.

"Hey, Deek." She was the one who'd tagged him back in high school. The silent shadow boy who'd moved in with his drunk of a dad for the last two years of school after his drug-addict mom had walked in front of a train somewhere out west. *Welcome to the South Bronx, sucker. Welcome to hell.* Her first words to him, her only words for a long time. He'd said nothing back, just watched her with that same unwavering scrutiny that he watched her with now.

He took a step over the threshold, then stepped back.

"Goddamn it, Deek. Get your ass in here and sit down," she waved at the folding steel chair beside her desk. Her office was just one in a long line of six-by-eight windowless plywood boxes each with an air vent. Hers was distinguished by a Xeroxed picture of the President the prior tenant had pinned up, complete with an evil Snidely Whiplash handlebar mustache and top hat, that she hadn't bothered to take down.

He finally cleared the threshold, inspected the four walls as if it was a trap about to spring shut on him, then stepped to the chair. He spun it around with a kick and sat on it backwards, resting his crossed arms on the seat back. His presence in her doorway had filled the small room. Now the geometry was placing him much too close to her.

She wondered if waiting him out was worth the effort. He looked like hell, in both meanings. He'd always been handsome as hell, which was all the more powerful because he never leveraged it. The closer girls flocked, the more he retreated. If there'd been a Loners Club back in school, she, Deek, and her brother would have ruled it.

He also looked sadder than she'd ever seen him. Which—

"Oh no! You're here about my Jimmy, aren't you?"

Deek nodded once but didn't speak.

"He's been dead two months. I saw the action report," she snapped a close-bitten nail against her computer screen, "before my commander brought the damned Chaplin in. What the hell took you so long? I'm not that hard to find."

She was a forward operations controller for North Africa Special Operations. Her posting at Camp Lemonnier, Djibouti, Horn of Africa—the only permanent US military base on the whole continent—made her damned easy to find. Deek must have been through here a half dozen times since that operation.

That operation. Her job was coordinating information flow for Special Operations teams assigned to AFRICOM—the US military's unified combatant command for all of Africa. She was the one who had placed the team on that roof. She hadn't issued the order, but she'd chosen the roof, mapped the access points, even arranged for their cars. Though she hadn't known which specific people went until the KIA list showed up at the end of the action report.

Sergeant James Borman. Killed in action (classified).

She hadn't even known until this moment that Deek had been there. In retrospect she supposed that it made perfect sense. Jimmy had been so excited the last time she saw him, assigned to work with Derek Davies after not seeing him once in the years since graduation—Deek had taken his diploma down to the Times Square recruiting station and signed up that day.

And now he must be hurting as badly as she was. Maybe that explained the two months.

He fished into the left breast pocket of his camo jacket

and pulled out a piece of paper. No, a photograph. He held it out by a corner trapped between the tips of two fingers. The office was so small that neither of them had to reach far for her to take it.

It was a picture of her, one that had been folded in half. She unfolded the other half though she already knew what she'd see.

Derek.

Making a goofy smile for the camera. No, for Jimmy, who was taking the photo. It was the only time that she'd ever seen him smile happily, and she'd only seen this one in the photo—not in real life.

She closed her eyes to block out Deek's bright smile of ten years ago and the dark and steady gaze of the top Delta Force sniper sitting across from her today. She hadn't cried at the news. She'd refused to cry. It was enough of a surprise that he hadn't died in high school— the South Bronx was a dangerous as hell place to grow up. Even more for a boy like Jimmy. He'd made it out, mostly due to Deek. And done well, until—

A hand took hers, shocking her into opening her eyes and staring at Deek.

"He didn't do anything wrong. Not one damned thing," Deek's voice was no more than a soft growl.

Cindy searched for something neutral to say, some way through the pain that ripped at her heart—an organ she'd carefully isolated and buried long ago. Especially around Deek.

"He was my guard. Sniper caught him. Single round from an unexpected angle. Damned good shot." He grunted the last as a grudging compliment.

Cindy clawed for a breath and managed to gasp out, "Did you get him?" Even though she knew it from the action report, she needed to know, to hear it. Now. From Deek's own mouth.

Deek nodded. "Him. And his spotter."

"Good!" It was all she could manage. She wished Deek would let go of her hand because she didn't have enough willpower to remove it on her own. The warm comfort was both sustaining her and battering down the walls of defense that an abusive father had helped her build. Abuse that she'd accepted in order to protect her little brother from further humiliation. It had continued all through her childhood and teens until one day it had suddenly stopped and he'd never touched her again. Nor had he gone back to abusing Jimmy. Somehow, they were suddenly free.

"That photo," he nodded down toward her other hand. "It's all he had on him."

"Never was much for writing letters or even e-mails," she managed, then looked down at the photo to look away from Deek. "That was a good day."

And it had been. The three of them had taken the D-train all the way down to Central Park and spent the day pretending they were high-rollers. Riding the carousel. Eating ice cream as they walked through the Central Park Zoo. Watching the rich people race their model sailboats on the "Conservatory Water"—that name had made them all laugh, as if it was too important to be called a pond.

Jimmy had gotten the camera so close in their faces that she and Deek had to crowd together and there was no room for the background around the edges. She could still remember how Deek's hand had felt tight around her waist. He was still the only man ever whose touch didn't give her at least a brief jolt of the creeps. Nobody was as safe to be around as Derek Davies.

"I remember every single minute," Deek's dark eyes studied her closely. Then he raised a hand and brushed her hair back in a soft caress.

For a moment she was lost in it, the breathtaking gentleness from such a hard man. The warm brush of his fingertips as he tucked her hair around the back of her ear. She could—

3

———

"Don't!" Cindy's snapped command had Deek jerking back his fingers as if they'd been burned.

"What? What did I do?"

"Nothing," but her arms were clenched so tightly about her chest he was afraid she would shatter. "Just don't touch me like that."

"Okay." But he'd always wanted to touch her like that. He'd only ever held her once, that single moment captured in Jimmy's damned photograph. It was the day he'd taken them to Central Park to celebrate—the day after he'd convinced their father that there were worse things than dying if he ever touched either of his children again.

All the women he'd ever been with, he'd ended up wishing they were Cindy Borman instead. Not one of them had been able to purge her wholly from his thoughts.

She was the standard that no one could ever live up to.

When he'd learned the strength she'd had, what she'd done to protect her brother, he'd been utterly humbled. That was the moment he'd fallen in love. Dopey-ass word, but it was the only one that fit. She'd gone from being the only girl he was friends with, to his personal definition of righteous strength.

Ever since then, he'd done his best to match her standard, though no way was he ever going to pull that off.

Sitting here in her plywood cube in boots, camo pants, and tan t-shirt, he'd never seen anything so incredible. He'd watched her work for five, maybe ten minutes before she'd noticed him. He had barely been able to breathe during that entire time. Her blond hair, no longer in a Jennifer Aniston shoulder-length style, was breathtaking chopped off at jaw-level. It was more… her. Her blue eyes now watched him, wide with…fear?

"What is it?"

She just shook her head, leaving him no guide signs for what to say next. He reached out and took her hand again, peeling it free from where it clenched her other arm. She wasn't fighting him, it was just as if she couldn't let go. He clamped her fine fingers between his two hands. He could feel her pulse racing where his finger lay against the inside of her wrist.

"Breathe, Cind."

"Can't!" It was a hard gasp.

"C'mon," he coaxed her. "You pass out on me and we're going to have a situation on our hands. I'm a shooter not a medic. I was so crappy I barely made it through the training." Combat first aid was a part of every

Delta's training. He didn't need to have gone for the extra year of medic training to see that she was panicking. Even if he didn't have a damned clue why.

She nodded in agreement but didn't relax. Had she been holding the hurt of Jimmy's loss inside her all this time? Closest thing he'd ever had to a little brother; it hurt like hell. She must be feeling it times ten.

At a loss, he just held onto her hand, imagining he was driving heat into it, though how her fingers could be so cold in the scorching summer of Djibouti he didn't know. It was over a hundred outside and the air-con vent was a joke.

"I really miss the little shit."

She barked out a laugh which was closer to a breath. "He really loved you."

Deek nodded, at a loss for what else to do. The big brother worship had been clear and he'd ended up liking it despite himself. He'd protected both of them when they were kids, and had been cool playing Delta Big Brother to Little Brother Ranger for that month before Jimmy went down. They never talked about the past— except one mention that Cindy was with AFRICOM at Camp Lemonnier—but Jimmy was an easy guy to be around. Deek had liked keeping a protective eye on him —right until the moment he'd fucked up and let Jimmy die.

He knew that wasn't true. The sniper had been well trained. Good enough that they'd sent in a Delta team to clear him out.

So it only felt like it was his fault that Jimmy had gone

down, even though he knew—and the mission review team agreed—that it wasn't.

He closed his eyes and raised Cindy's hand to press his cheek against the back of it. Even if it was just for a moment, he had to feel her touching him. For one little instant, he'd believe that it was somehow possible that—

"What are you doing?" She yanked her hand free.

She'd never let him touch her, except that one fine day.

He stood up. Right. Nothing here for him.

He braced himself in the doorway, but didn't turn to look at her when he spoke.

"I'm sorry I couldn't protect him better."

"If he died with you at his side, at least he was happy."

"Uh-huh," he couldn't make the next step off the threshold. He knew if he walked away from Cindy now, he'd never be able to face her again.

But—

"Wait. What?" He looked back at her over his shoulder, still holding onto the doorframe. A battered metal desk, a big computer screen, and the most beautiful woman who could never be his.

"He loved you so much."

"You said that already."

"It's true."

Deek thought about that for a moment. "Guess I loved him too."

"You guess?" Her sadness flashed into fury as she jolted to her feet and strode the three steps to face him.

He turned and looked down at her. Not far. He'd

forgotten how tall she was for a woman. Five ten of powerful soldier.

"You guess!" Her fair complexion was turning a mean red. He'd also forgotten that she had a temper—nothing ever phased her brother. He'd go quiet sometimes, but that was all. Cindy? Never any doubt what she was feeling. The only question was—would it hurt.

Apparently a shrug wasn't the right answer as she pummeled the side of her fist against his chest.

"Derek!" No one used his full name. It sounded foreign, even from Cindy.

"He..." Deek started to shrug again then thought better of it. "Jimmy was the best little brother anybody could want."

"I'm talking about *you*, not me," Cindy's voice sounded as if she was trying to talk to a dumb child and he didn't much like it.

"He was like a little brother to me too."

4

———

"He was..." Cindy stumbled over the words and almost tripped into Deek's chest. "He loved you."

"You keep saying that. I know it already. I'm not some dumb Jarhead. I'm Delta."

Cindy could only stare up at him, "Jimmy *loved* you, Deek."

"I know that!" His voice lowered dangerously.

"Oh my god," she stumbled back from Deek's dark frown. "He never told you. But I assumed you were—"

"Never told me what?"

No. This could *not* have landed in her lap to do. It wasn't fair. It wasn't possible. If her brother was still alive, she'd kill him. Right here. Right now.

"Cind?" He'd followed her back into the room though she didn't recall retreating until she'd collapsed back into her chair once more.

"Jimmy...was never interested in women. And there was only one man that he ever loved."

Deek blinked twice, then dropped into his own chair, facing her once more.

She waited. To be a Delta Operator meant that he was damned smart. A different kind of intelligence than hers maybe, not one that earned straight As in boring high school classes and everything else since then, but damned sharp.

"Oh shit!" It took him less than five seconds. "He never told me."

"You're seriously telling me that you didn't know?"

His abrupt laugh snapped out like a slap to the face. "He's not my type, Cind."

"Then who is?"

Deek's thin sheen of humor switched off as if it had never been. His dark eyes stared straight at her. Being a man of few words, he slowly raised one finger and pointed it at the center of her chest.

5

DEEK CONTINUED HIS KILLER WORKOUT ALL THROUGH THE hot afternoon. The obstacle course was busy with a whole team of swabbies getting their land-side workout and he didn't want to have to eat their dust—something the whole damned country specialized in. Instead he'd eat his own. Delta often fought solo, and he was fine sweating solo. Nobody pushed an operator harder than himself.

Besides, he needed to be alone and do some serious thinking.

He found a tractor tire no one else was using along the back fence of the Special Ops compound and set up a workout. Fifty flips of the five hundred pound tire. Then a hundred agility hops into and onto the tire—first both feet, then right foot only, then left only, coming to a stable stop in each position. Then fifty crunches, sitting on one edge of the tire with his feet hooked into the far side—a fifty-pound weight on his chest as he lay back until his head touched the ground, then back up.

By the fourth complete rep his mind finally cleared enough that he could review what had happened.

Cindy had thrown him out. Only one word, "Leave!" and her own pointing finger jammed in the direction of the door.

Like the dog he was, he'd tucked his tail and run.

But it didn't make any sense. How was he supposed to know that Jimmy liked guys? Or liked him...that way? He knew it happened. This was the new, enlightened military. And that and ten cents didn't buy you a stick of gum. There was another stupid phrase. Had anyone ever sold gum by the stick? Must have, he supposed. But enlightened military? Yeah, right. No wonder Jimmy had gone so kick-ass tough.

Deek knocked back a bottle of water and went back to flipping the tractor tire up and down the brown packed-dirt stretch behind Task Command's CHUs. The containerized housing units rose three stories high and were exclusively for the use of Special Operations teams. His present home, as much as he ever had one, was third row, second tier, fourth from the left.

Here behind the last row, the waste heat of all the individual air conditioners raised the temperature another five or ten degrees but at least they put out some damned moisture into the air, a few extra percent anyway. It also had the advantage of isolation. No one except security patrols wandered back here because the security fence which cut off the SOF compound from the rest of the camp stood only a few meters away. Any grunts out in the main camp wanted to watch him flip a tire, they were welcome to—he had nothing to do with them.

Deek supposed that Jimmy's actions made some kind of sense. Deek had never seen him with a girl. But then again...the three of them were total loners in high school. Deek still had been until Jimmy was assigned to his detail. He didn't know about Cindy, but there hadn't been a single picture in her office other than the Command-in-Chief's, such as it was.

Jimmy had always hung close to Deek when he had a chance. On the long quiet watches, he'd act as if he had something to say, but never did. And now Deek knew what it was.

Poor kid.

But that still didn't explain Cindy's reaction, sending him off like that.

His ears were starting to ring from the repeated thumps of the big tire on the hard earth. His muscles were well past burn and deep into sear. It felt good. It felt familiar. Another couple full reps and he'd go down to the rifle range to work on his accuracy while going through lactic acid withdrawal. He drank back half a bottle of water, dumped the rest on his head, turning the dust that coated him into mud, then chucked it aside and picked up the fifty pound weight.

Cindy had looked really pissed. Like some goddess of fury come to life. And he still didn't know why.

"You're a smart guy, Deek," he lay back then grunted himself upward to start another set of deep crunches with the weight on his chest.

"Figure it out." Crunch.

"She's mad because..." That lasted him through five more crunches without finding the next word.

"She's mad because..." he grunted upward again and froze.

Cindy was standing not ten feet away. Feet planted, arms crossed.

The fifty-pound weight he'd been clutching to his chest overbalanced him and took him down again. Coming back up from that one was hard. Once he was back up, he dumped the weight to the side and just looked at her.

She still looked absolutely amazing. Not the most beautiful girl in any crowd, but when you knew the person inside...nobody else stood a chance.

And he was sweaty, muddy, probably stank like a workout, and his breathing was so ragged that he was getting lightheaded just watching her.

Cindy stepped forward and, after he pulled in his legs, stepped into the tire and sat across the circle from him. Their knees were only inches apart. He leaned over for another two liter water bottle and their knees brushed together. He pulled his in closer and she did the same.

Guzzling down half the water did nothing for his parched throat.

"She...doesn't know why she's so mad," Cindy finally said softly.

"Huh." Deek couldn't think of anything else to say.

6

IT WAS ALL JUMBLED UP INSIDE HER. SHE HAD TRIED GOING back to her data, but it was a low priority research project that she still had a couple days on before it was needed. It hadn't been enough to draw her focus. Cindy had thought about going for a run...and had come to half an hour later still staring at her locked computer screen.

There was no way she could eat.

She didn't have any really close friends on base, didn't have any that she could call either. It was like when she found out her brother had died. No one to tell. No one to care.

Except for the man sitting across from her.

He hadn't been hard to find. She'd just followed the tortured grunts of someone working past their limits, but not acknowledging they had any limits to begin with. Nothing ever stopped Deek. Nothing.

"I didn't know," he finally said softly. "I swear I didn't."

"Neither did I."

He narrowed his eyes at her.

"I knew about Jimmy," her voice drifted softer. "I didn't know about you."

He nodded.

But there was more. Her assumptions weren't the only reason she hadn't tried to crack Derek Davies's loner shell. Who could want a girl who had chosen to be raped by her father? Even if it was to protect her brother. Nobody. That's who. Certainly not the only person she'd ever told about it. Jimmy had to know, to have understood. But he'd never let on. Some things were better never spoken about.

Whereas Deek...

"Oh my god. You're the one who stopped him."

"Your dad? Damn straight."

That took a second to sink in. Another thing she'd never known. Derek—Deek no longer sounded right to her—had protected both her and her brother. She covered her face for a long moment. How could she not have known? It was so obvious now that she thought about. "Friends" had been too strong a word for what they were, but they were *all* each other had in those times. She looked back up at him, unsure of what she'd see. But he still looked like the same, dirty, sweaty, amazing man he'd always been. Maybe a *lot* dirtier and sweatier than usual.

He shrugged his shoulders, not in a denying way, but rather as if he wished he could do it again. In retrospect she was surprised that Derek hadn't killed him outright. He'd certainly had the strength to.

"The photograph. That day." She'd never connected that either. "That was the day it all stopped."

He nodded and drank some more water.

"You said it was a day of celebration. That's why you smiled like that."

He looked aside for a long moment. "I did that for Jimmy. So that he'd know it was over. It was harder on him than you. He was never half as strong as you are. Maybe that's what made him try so hard as a Ranger, trying to make up for what he couldn't do as a kid. I was trying to cheer him up."

"Whereas me..."

Again, the look aside.

This time she waited him out.

He finally looked back. "You I held. Even for that one moment, I just held you safe."

She didn't know what to say and didn't have the chance.

"I also wanted to feel how someone could be so strong. Could take so much shit and still be so incredible. I wanted to know what it felt like to be as good as you. And care about someone, *anyone,* as much as you did for Jimmy. That caring was never part of my life, but it shone out of you like the sun. I've spent every minute since trying to live up to that feeling."

Cindy laughed, "I think that's the longest speech of your entire life."

Derek shrugged, finished the water, and smiled at her. Not grinned, smiled. Not the goofy look he'd made for her brother's sake. This was genuine and deep.

"I'm not all that strong."

"Bullshit!" Now Derek grinned. "Ain't a heroine in the movies got an edge on you. They're strong on the outside. Hell, any idiot can do that."

He thumped a fist against the tire and she could feel the vibration of it through her tailbone.

"You've got it in here."

He tapped her chest—they were close enough for that to be easy, though he pulled back his hand quickly and might even have blushed a little.

"That's how I made Delta. Trying to be as strong as you on the *inside*."

Cindy's head was spinning. One of America's top warriors, trying to be as strong as her. As he imagined her. No, as he *believed* her to be.

The way Derek saw her was...incredible.

"I told myself I was angry at you for rejecting Jimmy. For not returning what he felt so deeply for you."

Her man of few words was back, twisting his neck until she could practically hear the crackle along his spine.

"And I know for a fact that I was angry as hell that he got you and I didn't."

"But—"

"Shut up, Derek." The name felt like a caress as she said it. As if she could finally acknowledge the man, rather than the boy she kept at a careful distance.

He shut up.

"I wish to god I could tell Jimmy that. Not that I ever let him see it. But I wish I could tell him that and let him know I'm not angry at him any more."

"You were the one thing Jimmy and I always agreed

on." Derek nodded as if talking to her brother right there, next around the circle on their tractor tire.

"What was that?"

"That you were the best woman on the planet."

"And you were both deluding yourselves." She wasn't any of that.

"Says you," again Derek smiled at her...for her...*because* of her. "From where I'm sitting," he thumped the tire again, "Jimmy and I had it dead to rights. Besides..."

He trailed off, then reached out to caress her cheek. This time she let him and could feel that impenetrable wall she'd built so high—so high that she barely knew herself—simply get brushed aside as if it had never been there.

"Besides," he repeated in a whisper as soft as his caress. "It's rude to argue with both a dead man and the man who loves you."

He pulled her in, with the lightest of pressure.

Derek leaned in to meet her halfway, but paused just before their lips touched, when she could see herself so clearly in his dark eyes. "There's only ever been you, Cindy."

She swallowed against the tears, the tears that hadn't spilled at Jimmy's death, that hadn't spilled since she was a little girl afraid in the dark.

She was no longer afraid. Could never be with Derek beside her.

"There's only ever been you, Derek," she whispered back as the tears flowed.

Who knew that all of the tears stored inside her heart were tears of joy.

HER SILENT HEART AND THE OPEN SKY

Delta Force operator Chris Cooper once again stands in the nightmare that is Helmand Province, Afghanistan. His mission: to remove the Taliban leadership, again.

Born in the Soviet-Afghan War, trained by the Mujahideen, and the Americans after them, Azadah believes her heart and hope are spent past return.

They must fight together if they hope to find Her Silent Heart and the Open Sky.

INTRODUCTION

In a collection filled with some of my favorite stories, as well as numerous fan favorites, this one still shines forth for me. It's why I saved it until last.

So many of the elements of Delta Force that I've mentioned before came together in this story: their silence, their adaptability, their drive to make it right, their complete disregard for how awful the environment might be if it gets the job done, and more.

It is also one of the few times I was able to squeeze a team into a short story. It made for one of the longest short stories I've ever written, almost double any of the other stories in this collection.

But I felt that it needed that space. We needed the expansiveness of this tale to see some of the things that weren't in the other stories: Delta's teamwork, their commitment to help, and their apparently casual connection that is as close as a family's, often closer.

I've studied a great deal about the elite special operations teams in our military, particularly: The Night

Stalkers, Delta Force, and SEAL Team 6. The one universal that connects these elite warriors is why they're there.

No matter what brought them to the fight originally, they stay for only one reason. Every single soldier or sailor (SEALs are sailors) at this level who plans to retire will say almost exactly the same thing: *I'll miss the team.*

They stayed in for the team. That is their family.

For the heroine Azadah, I wanted to look at some of the displacement, the pain that wars have perpetrated upon the local populations. I first went there with Dilya in Night Stalkers #2, *I Own the Dawn.*

Azadah didn't start out at the bottom as Dilya had. She'd had a life, a family, and a career. Only circumstances have now backed her into a corner where she was a cleaning woman and cook for a foreign military team—a role that she could easily be killed for if it was ever discovered.

This is Azadah's tale far more than it being a tale of Delta Force or war.

It is about never losing the ability to dream.

1

———

Lashkar Gah, the capital of Helmand Province, Afghanistan—was called the Capital of Hell during the War in Afghanistan. It was hard to believe he was back.

Delta Force operator Sergeant Chris "Deuce" Cooper surveyed the hovel that was their new home. Close by Bost Airport, the only thing it had going for it was it actually had a roof and all four walls. None of the other nearby structures could brag as much.

The insides didn't disappoint; they were equally meager. The walls were adobe, the roof stick, straw, and daubed mud. There wasn't enough rain here to wash it away, especially not in summer. A hundred-plus in the shade and no measurable rain for seven months.

Two small rooms were connected by an archway. It was surprisingly tidy, the hard-packed dirt floor had no buildup of sand from the notorious dust storms. In the front room a battered table, two benches, and three chairs with the backs broken off were neatly arranged. The second room—empty but clean and where they'd be sleeping—showed fresh sweeping marks and not a camel spider or scorpion in sight despite the cool shade.

The other five members of his team surged in out of the midday heat and began dumping heavy packs and bedrolls in the open room.

No one else paid any attention to the cleaning woman. She squatted in a small nook that had a smoky fireplace for burning cow dung and a spot only wide enough for the woman to squat while cooking or lie down and sleep, but not both. She clutched the bundle of bound twigs that was her broom like it was a lifeline— her knuckles white.

She barely looked up as they entered. At his greeting, she'd looked down once more. Abashed to be an Afghan woman alone with six American soldiers? Or too unintelligent to care? Perhaps a third option.

Command had told them they'd have local help which was a bonus. It meant they wouldnt't be living on MREs. She'd know how to shop and cook local chow and he was fine with that. Maxwell and Jaffe, fresh out of training, were new to the squad and it would take them some time squatting over the shitter to build up the right gut flora, but he and the other three operators had walked these roads before and were happy enough to eat local as long as it took no effort on their part.

For himself, a boy raised on pasta and beef in upstate New York, he looked forward to the Afghan cuisine. On previous tours he'd grown a taste for the clean, simple flavors of fresh-baked naan seed bread, rice with tomatoes or lamb and raisins, and Qorma stew. He hoped she was a good cook.

They'd been offered a bunkhouse at Camp Bastion-Leatherneck (now Camp Shorabak), but preferred to be outside anyone else's perimeter—especially the Afghan Armed Forces. They'd been labeled as advisors, but the form of "advice" they were bringing didn't include being in contact with the local forces.

He could see the others assess and forget the servant. Within days they'd think nothing of undressing and crawling into the sack while she puttered about. If she was offended, it would be up to her to leave the room.

"Nothing but wallpaper, man."

Except she wasn't.

Chris noticed that her head scarf was decorative and of the highest quality, or had once been. It was worn thin and time-faded, but it wasn't the scarf of the poorest classes. Its unusual shade of summer green still shone through. Her one vanity left from a former existence? Or stolen from an abandoned home, thoughtlessly left behind years ago by someone with enough money to flee? She posed a lot of questions for him if not for the others.

He didn't make a deal of it, but assigned himself first guard detail and kept an eye out.

She revealed herself in stages as the others sorted gear, shot the shit, and settled in after the long flight. They'd come in on the biweekly commercial flight in ones and twos dressed as Arab businessmen. They'd grabbed boxes from the cargo that hadn't looked related —their weapons had been in his box labeled as tractor parts. Conway's box was restaurant supply, a month of MREs that they could now not eat. Baxter and Burton smuggled in the comm and surveillance gear and Maxwell and Jaffe, being the new guys, were mainly loaded down with heavy rounds of ammunition and explosives.

As the guys settled, Chris noticed the woman didn't leave the room at random. Rather she found additional tasks until some story was complete: a story told in a language that she had pretended was gibberish to her.

And when she did move, it wasn't with the slow, painful moves of the crone that most of her attire suggested. Nor was it that of a teen. Their servant was a woman who understood English and was intent on keeping that knowledge to herself.

It took a full day before he managed to see her face as she consistently looked down and kept her scarf forward. Every now and then he'd catch her watching them, but she always looked away the moment he turned to face her. Unable to get a good view of her face, Chris settled on subterfuge, walking close by her and dropping a spoon.

He squatted directly in front of her as she reached for it. Her face—damn but this woman had a face. Clear skin brushed golden-brown, prominent cheekbones, and strong eyebrows that only emphasized the clear dark eyes. The hand that returned the spoon was dirty, but strong and unlined.

He almost said, "Thank you" in Pashto, but at the last moment he switched from *"Ddera manena"* to the Dari *"Tashakor,"* Something about the strength of her face perhaps, or the fullness of her tightly closed mouth.

"Qabele tashakor nest." She looked shocked by her own

"You're welcome." She too had spoken in Dari rather than offering the more likely *"Har kela"* in Pashto. Her voice was warm and smooth, with just a little roughness as if she used it only rarely.

In an eyeblink she was gone, not just from the room, but from the house.

Her response meant Dari was probably her native tongue. That would place her home in northern Afghanistan, if she was even Afghani. How had the poor woman ended up in the desert of the far south as a servant? There was no worse place that the country had to offer than Helmand Province. He knew. He'd fought in most of them.

2

Azadah stood by the well, but had brought no water container.

She could go to the market, but it was a long walk and she had just gone this morning to prepare for the American's arrival. It wouldn't matter; the stalls would now be closed in the heat of midday. She had paid a bribe to get the position—a bribe that was only shocking in how meager it had needed to be. How far she had fallen, nothing left but her clothing and her pride.

She stared out at the empty airport. It shimmered in the dry heat. The place where so many planes used to land that there was never silence in Lashkar Gah was now filled only with the wind and the one lone passenger plane that would be leaving soon. That plane was the only safe way to cross back to Kandahar or Kabul—if one had the money. The roads were filled with Afghan checkpoints, Taliban ambushes, and shifting sands.

The American Air Force had staged here and supplied the Marine Corps troops stationed at the great camp north of the city. The British too had been here. They had tried to bring peace. Instead they had given the Taliban a focus and Lashkar Gah had been shredded time after time between the two forces. Now the Taliban came and the Afghan Armed Forces fought them off, but there was little enthusiasm on either side.

But the Americans were back.

There were so few of them, what could they think to accomplish here?

And by asking the question, she knew.

Azadah tipped her head back to look at the skies wondering if she could see it. She couldn't, but didn't doubt that it was there. A drone, impossibly small and far away, circled somewhere above them. Was it looking down at her right now?

"They're very hard to spot," a voice said close behind her.

She looked back down from the sky and was momentarily dizzy. The one they called "Deuce," the one who had tricked her into speaking, had put on a *shalwar kameez*. In the linen drawers and long body shirt, he looked almost native. His beard was short and neat, his hair dark. Only the light brown of his eyes seemed out of place. They were as light as the desert at dusk.

"But they can see us?" Only after she spoke did she realize that again he had tricked her. He had spoken in English and she had replied in the same language.

She had not been caught in years. The last time had earned her a crashing hard slap across the face from an Afghan guard and three months in a prison cell while they debated whether or not to shoot her for spying. The

Americans had freed her only when they were recalled back to their country and she could no longer be a threat to them. For a time she feared they would forget about her at the last minute, or perhaps remember. In the end it was as if the three months of her life became nothing.

Azadah prepared to run toward the market, not that she had much hope of losing herself there. Even the watching eye above them would not be needed. She had seen that the man was fleet of foot and he was most certainly armed. This one would have at least three weapons with him: ankle, hip, and at the center of his belly where he could draw it so fast that all she could see was a blur when he did so. He did not have his rifle with him for all of the good it would do her.

But he did not reach for her. He did not slip a hand into his clothing to hold a weapon. He did not appear smug about uncovering her secret. Instead he stood quietly and watched her, waiting until she spoke again.

"What is Deuce? I do not know this word."

"Deuce? It is a playing card for a game with two markers on it. My initials are C. C., Chris Cooper, and they called me that at first. Then 'Two C.' On my third mission, the situation got a little ugly. I solved it by killing two people with one bullet. Luck as much as anything. 'Two C.' became 'Deuce' and it stuck."

His casual tone reassured her as much as anything. "I don't think luck has much to do with your life."

His shrug said maybe. "I met you."

"I work here."

"You are also at the wrong end of your country and speak excellent English."

Not knowing what else to say, Azadah repeated herself, "I work here." These were more words than she had spoken in any language in a year and it was exhausting.

"Who do you work for is the next question."

Security. It is always security. Her country no longer spoke of the seasons or the crops. There was less concern for the next dust storm or the birth of a child than of who was aligned with who. There was only, always, security. She was sick of it.

"I speak to no one."

"You're speaking to me. I guess that makes me no one," he managed to sound hurt.

And she almost smiled, but she was too out of practice. "Yes, it is as I said. I speak to *no one*. I work here."

"Cleaning?"

"Yes."

"And cooking?"

"Yes, and carrying water."

"Which you must carry in your cupped palms," he pointed at her empty hands.

"And I watch men itch and scratch while they have nothing to do," she shot back at him, piqued at being caught. She did not like that he knew exactly how much he had surprised her.

"I'm talking to you. That counts as doing something."

Azadah stared at him for a long moment. This man they called Two C.—she did not like the way "Deuce" felt on her tongue—*was* talking to her. He was not interrogating her. He had not struck her or arrested her.

He was *talking* to her. He already knew more about her than she had revealed to anyone in a long time.

Did he somehow also know that her parents had fled Iran during the fall of the Shah and their great mistake had been fleeing to the east? They had arrived in Afghanistan at the same time as the Russians. She'd been born in the midst of "Russia's Vietnam," a fifteen-year disaster for both countries in which a million Afghan civilians were killed and six million fled their homeland entirely.

Rushing to the relative safety of the mujahideen, they had served as skilled administrators. The American-backed rebels' success against the Russians had come to nothing when the tribes then fell to fighting among themselves.

Then Mohammed Omar had taken those hard-learned fighting skills and leftover American weaponry and formed the Taliban. Another half-million Afghans had died, including her parents, before Osama bin Laden's bombing of New York had forced the Americans to face what they had helped create.

In each incarnation, Azadah's lot had slipped lower and lower. She'd been born to senior government officials. She'd grown up in the administration centers of a nationwide insurgency. She had cowered during the rule of the Taliban as a clerk; invaluable because she knew everyone and every connection, reviled because of her sex.

And now she had become a cleaner and cook for this man.

He was not a big man, no more than any Afghan. She

was tall for a woman and only had to look upward a hand's width when speaking with him.

"Why are you here, Two C.? Why have you Americans come back?"

His smile acknowledged her preference for his older nickname. He pointed to the scant shade afforded by the side of a house. There was no roof and through the windows there was only rubble—a casualty of the 2008 Taliban bombardment of the city. She couldn't remember the family who'd lived there and that bothered her. It was as if she'd just become disconnected from her own country.

She followed him there out of the sun. She'd forgotten how much the Americans hated the heat and the brightness. He did not stand too close. It wouldn't be right. If she were anybody, she might be shunned by the community for even speaking with a lone male—and if the Taliban were in control she might be beaten or even killed—but she wasn't and for the moment they weren't, so perhaps it didn't matter.

"We are here," he told her once they were settled, "because the Taliban see the weaknesses in the Afghan Armed Forces as opportunity. We have learned that great force is not the answer here. It was me and people like me who cut the head off the snake. We have come to do it again."

Azadah leaned back against the wall suddenly tired of it all. She had fought so long, her family had given so much, and once more they had come full circle.

This man from a land so foreign she could scarcely

imagine it had left his home and come back to Afghanistan.

"The head of this snake will always grow anew." Perhaps he heard the resignation in her voice, the hopeless battle that was Afghanistan. Her country had once been rich in art and literature, if not money. Now, after forty years of war, the country barely had buildings.

"Then," Two C. said with a calm confidence that forced her to look back at his quiet face. "We will come back and cut it off again."

3

———

CHRIS KNEW NOT TO TRUST A PRETTY FACE—NO MATTER how goddamn striking—he hadn't joined the service just yesterday.

But he considered himself a better than average judge of human character, and there were things about his woman that didn't fit together. At least not if she was a spy, infiltrator, or saboteur.

"May I ask your name?"

"Azadah. So true, is it not?" Despite her obvious soul-deep weariness, she was still capable of humor.

Her name: independent, free.

She struck him as a woman trapped...but not subdued. *Qawi* perhaps. The word meant both strong and powerful. But *manda* as well, so weary that she could scarce stand under her own weight.

He'd done many tours in Iraq and Afghanistan. Handled more than a few operations in places better not mentioned beyond the borders of Iran and Pakistan. In some places no Arab woman would think to speak with him.

Yet Azadah spoke with him. And she showed of herself who she was.

"I'm inclined to trust you, Azadah."

"I am trustworthy," she said without looking at him. "Or I was. Now I no longer know. I do what I do."

He too leaned back against the mud wall to look out across the area. This whole section of houses had been abandoned. Storms had piled the dust in odd drifts against the few remaining walls. But, like any poor culture, anything that could be salvaged had been. There was little waste, merely the tan-dusted wreckage of what had once been a community.

The city of Lashkar Gah had grown from two-hundred thousand to two-fifty over the last decade, but still that had not been enough to push people back into this ravaged corner of the older city. Dating back a thousand years, the city's ill-fated name translated as "Army Barracks" and described only too well its war-torn history.

The brush of a breeze invaded their bit of stolen shade with a slap of heat that experience told him he would never fully adapt to in their time here.

"The place I come from is a land of water and trees," he didn't know quite why he was telling her this. "It is called the Finger Lakes and is in the far west of our New York State. The lakes are long, thin, and spread like a hand. The country is so beautiful that the local tribes said it was where God rested his hand after finishing creation." He could almost see it, laid like a green mirage over the desolate land before him.

She did not answer for a very long time. When she did, her words were almost a soft caress.

"Thank you. I can almost see your land of green. It is good to believe such places exist."

And then, in that way she had, Azadah was gone and he stood alone in the shrinking wedge of shade formed by a broken wall.

4

———

THREE DAYS LATER CHRIS FOUND A SLIP OF PAPER ON HIS pillow. It lay so close to his nose that it should have tickled.

It was an address and a name. A name that had him sitting up sharply and not bothering to wonder how the paper had arrived there without him waking. Abdullah bin Hazar wasn't at the top of their target list, but he wasn't at the bottom either.

Chris snapped his fingers and the rest of the team came awake. Maxwell had been on guard, in between predictable trips to the shitter. Somehow he too had missed the delivery of the slip of paper. Because, Chris knew, no one but him saw Azadah, now a fixture in their midst.

She had been so stealthy that she hadn't disturbed his sleep, which made him uncomfortable. He preferred the idea that she was already a familiar presence in his mind so that his unconscious vigilance had let her come so close. They had not spoken again, but he couldn't help tracking her movements whenever she was in or near the building. She revealed the depth of their mutual awareness when he would glance around unexpectedly and find her watching him. At first, her gaze had flinched away, but just last night she had watched him for a long moment before, he'd swear, she'd blushed and looked down.

Rather than show the slip of paper around as it would cause too many questions, he jumped straight in.

"The third building to the south of the road to Marjeh, close by the Helmand River. Get me everything we know."

The team snapped to. In moments they had the drone retasked and feeding them images. A small compound less than a kilometer away, it would be overlooking the river if not for its high wall.

"I've got three late-model SUVs out front and four armed guards," Conway reported. The "Con Man" had been Chris' right-hand man through some ugly shit and, as usual, was hunched over the drone controls. They couldn't actually fly the thing from here, those guys lived in a hole in Nevada, but they could take over the camera feed and streaming video archive as needed.

Three new SUVs. Not unheard of, but certainly not common in this city.

"I have cell transmissions," Baxter reported.

"Who doesn't these days?" Burton countered.

The two of them were like a Laurel and Hardy routine; never just one spoke. They'd been collectively tagged as "BB" because they would sometimes chatter back and forth like a BB gun plinking away at tin cans.

"CIA at Langley has squat." "Try The Activity." "Duh! Already on it!" The two of them were one of the sharpest electronic surveillance teams in the business.

Chris let the sound of his team working the problem blend into the background. He was watching the silent woman who lay unmoving on the floor before the hearth. She was curled up with her shawl pulled over her face as she typically did while sleeping. Her hand clutched her shawl tightly as it always did, as if it was her last sliver of hope. But now her breathing was different. He watched the uneven acceleration of the movement of her ribcage.

"The Activity has nothing." "Cell transmissions are not in the clear."

Encrypted signals. They were getting smarter about not being overheard. He knew Baxter would route them to Burton to send back for possible decryption.

"Running back the video," Conway was on it. The drone had a camera system that could see the entire width and length of the city. The resolution was so high they could zoom in on a small area like the compound, and then roll time backwards.

"Two SUVs were on the move three hours ago. One traces to another compound on the northeast side of the city, but the second one had arrived from the direction of Kandahar to the east. Close-ups coming in."

Chris moved up to sit on the bunk next to Jaffe who was working the current drone feed rather than the historic one. But he managed to align himself so that a darkened screen reflected the "sleeping" Azadah. Moments after he turned his back, she indeed raised a lazy hand to remove her shawl. *Couldn't resist looking, could you?*

Chris glanced over his shoulder to let her know she'd been caught. Rather than a blush, she met his gaze for three long heartbeats.

She was watching him. Waiting to see what he would do with the information she'd provided. Had she set a trap for them?

For perhaps the first time in his whole military career he was going to consciously choose to engage an unknown area on the advice of an unknown civilian. He only knew her name, her beauty, and her weariness. *If you're an agent, you're damn good at your job, lady.*

She made no reply to his unspoken thought, instead turned away to tend the low fire.

In half an hour they had the compound clearly in their heads and a plan of action. His core team knew the faces of all of the main players on their target, but he made sure they reviewed Abdullah bin Hazar's photo again. He assigned the new guys to backup roles until he had a better feel for them.

They'd already scouted and acquired several vehicles. Bost Airport was like a junkyard. Cars left behind by departing businessmen. Trucks that were too worn for the evacuating US forces to bother taking or permanently disabling. They'd spent the last few days putting together a small but serviceable fleet of unremarkable appearance.

Once ready, they dispatched out of the building. It would be twilight soon. They'd leave now and do some daytime scouting. Then they'd wait for nightfall and slide in from three directions at once.

Chris let the others go out, then stepped over to the kitchen from which Azadah hadn't reemerged. She was waiting for him, he could tell even though she still squatted with her back turned.

"Abdullah?" He asked, meaning far more than confirming their target.

She nodded without turning.

"You'll still be here when we get back." He was careful to not make it a question.

Again her nod, then so softly that he could barely hear her, "I have nowhere else to go."

He left her there and followed his men out into the yard.

"Hitting on the maid servant, Deuce?" Conway teased him as Chris slid into the driver's seat of a ten-year old silver Toyota Corolla. It was a small and awkward car to launch an attack from if they were surprised, but over half of the cars on the road were aged Corollas, so it was as good as invisible.

"Looking to be put into an early grave, Conway?" Azadah wasn't the sort of woman who a man just yanked down her *partug* and took from behind. One look in her eyes told him that. Easy women existed. Even in a conservative place like this country, there were plenty of willings, both unpaid and paid. Azadah was not one of them.

"Well, now that you—"

"Just drive!"

5

AZADAH STARED INTO THE SMALL FIRE AND WONDERED AT the enormity of what she'd done. The two cars and a truck had departed and the echoing silence of the evening settled over the house.

For three days the six men had been constantly here, at least some of them. She'd never been alone except during the short walk to the well or the long walk to market. Often they went out in ones or twos on lazy "patrols," ambling along just like any local. But she'd heard the reports when they returned and how they were familiarizing themselves with an impressive amount of detail about the city. Two hundred thousand people in a rectangular area roughly three by five kilometers, yet they soon knew it as well as many who had spent their lives here.

Now, there was only her own breathing, the bleating of a distant goat, and the silence that was Afghanistan.

She...liked Two C. She liked her own joke of calling him that, partly because the man Chris was overwhelming. She'd seen how the others followed him, always wanting his good opinion, asking his advice. These warriors, America's very best, respected him deeply and listened carefully when he spoke.

It was rare for him to speak first which she also liked about him. He too understood the value of listening.

That was how she'd heard about Abdullah. A chance comment in the market had led her to walk far across the city and listen as she followed a goat that wasn't hers by the compound's gates in the great stone wall.

She knew this once had been an American city, even called "Little America" by some. They had come during the Cold War and built dams and waterways to create a massive irrigation system across the surrounding desert. They had built roads, homes, swimming pools...all of which had ultimately failed. Some farming occurred here, but the great agricultural plenty promised in the 1950s and 60s had been gone long before the Russians invaded in the late 1970s. Instead, the open-plan American style of buildings had been closed in after they left with three-meter high walls.

One of these had been taken over by Taliban leader Abdullah bin Hazar.

But why had she told the Delta Force soldier?

Why had she exposed herself to hope once more?

It was a question she had not answered when the twilight fell, nor when the men returned just hours before the dawn.

She listened to the footsteps. There was an excitement. There was an energy in the air that she'd forgotten the feeling of. There was a slap of weary bodies collapsing onto thick bedrolls as the soldiers dropped down on them. Weapons rattled.

One set of footsteps crossed to the threshold that separated the sleeping and the kitchen area. They stopped there, unmoving.

Azadah reached out to nurse the fire back to life and to begin the cooking of breakfast.

The meal was nearly ready before she heard the footsteps move away.

6

———

"I want Syed!" Jaffe growled as he slammed down his gear.

It wasn't even worth responding. They all wanted him, Chris most of all. Their three-month tour was up in just a few more days and the Taliban leader for all of Helmand had eluded them so far.

He had been there. Even during the first operation when they'd taken down Abdullah and a local lieutenant. While they'd been scouting the compound, one of the three Range Rovers had departed. Not knowing who was in it, they had let it go. When Chris finally gave the team the go, Abdullah had died in the first round. But before his lieutenant bled out he reported that Syed Harim Akhram had indeed been there earlier and just left.

Three months they had been chasing him back and forth across the countryside, twice over the ninety miles to Kandahar but with no success.

After their initial success with Abdullah, command had taken a real interest in their operation. A heavier drone had been lofted with more sophisticated communications detection and an even better camera. Computing assets had been layered in behind that to intercept and interpret cell and radio communications in real time.

For three months they had become a jacked-up, head-of-snake-eradicating machine. Three of the senior-level people, along with dozens of minor ones, had been tracked and taken down due to the millions of dollars of effort.

Yet five other top Taliban leaders had been taken down by tiny slips of paper left on his pillow while he slept through the heat of the day. He didn't know Azadah's wages, but assumed it was typical for the region, a hundred Afghanis. A dollar and a half a day.

Also for three months, they had barely spoken again. Only when the day was done and the first stars shone across the desert sky, sometimes she would come and sit by him. He'd imagine they were looking over a different landscape, one of rolling green hills, grazing cows, and cool forest. He would grill lamb and chicken Spiedie kebabs and would serve them to her in a fold of sesame-seed crusted Italian scali bread as the sky faded and the stars ruled the summer sky.

More than once he fell asleep with his back propped against the wall and his feet crossed together on the sand, listening to her silence. But he always woke alone, never hearing her leave.

7

THREE DAYS!

Azadah had never felt so helpless. They would be gone in three days and she would be...lost. How was one woman's heart supposed to hold so many emotions?

She shouldn't care!

Others had come and gone. So why did these men tear at her so?

They had been thoughtlessly kind to her and she would miss them. They had eaten heartily of the food she'd made them and occasionally even thought to thank her.

Five of them had treated her so.

But the sixth—

Unable to stand the thought, she snatched her market basket and fled from the house.

They had done exactly as Two C. had promised; they had cut the head off the snake, or at least most of it. She had seen no prisoners, heard of none. Maybe the

Americans had finally learned that a dead terrorist was far simpler than a live one.

She knew Syed plagued them and twice she'd heard almost enough to find him, but not quite. Not without exposing herself more than she dared.

No one knew about "her men" as she'd come to think of them. People certainly knew what they were doing though. She could see the effect in the way the Afghan Armed Forces had increased their patrols through the city. As she made her way into the market she could see that they held their heads a little higher. People even waved at them on occasion as if it was their doing. The heavy mantle that was the Taliban was once again lifting its smothering weight from the city. Maybe this time it would even be enough.

But her men were leaving.

Worse, her *man* was leaving.

In her panic, her feet had carried her to the edge of the market, for where else had she to go. She slowed and joined the others in the lazy heat, but her mind would not settle.

How would a day be without Chris "Two C." Cooper to smile at her when he was pleased? How could she possibly wake up and not see him there, sleeping so close by her that she felt like she existed, like she mattered once more? And perhaps worst of all, to never again sit beside him as evening fell and feel the peace inside the man, no matter his duty of death?

She had been invisible for so long that it should be easy to go back to her old habits. But not this time. He saw her in a way no one ever had before. And she saw him so clearly. His effortless leadership. His simple rough brand of kindness that made his men both respect and trust him.

How could she—

And then she heard it.

An old serving woman who she recognized as Abdullah bin Hazar's cook, the woman who had unwittingly led her to that first discovery. She was complaining of the load she must carry and the food she must cook. It was a common complaint heard about the market, especially when a feast was planned. But who was she cooking for now? There was no holy feast day coming.

Once a trusted servant of the Taliban, always one?

Perhaps. Just perhaps.

She did what she could to keep within listening range. She studied the pretty dye powders while the woman bought cauliflower and onion. She inspected the scrawny chickens on offering while the woman bought a lamb and drank tea while it was slaughtered and the meat was dressed.

Azadah did not have to stay too close as the woman's complaints were not soft.

"With no warning. Big guest coming to town. Many people."

Azadah wanted to follow, but how to do so discreetly?

"Very important man. Very important guests."

And that was when Azadah made her mistake. She stood in one place watching for too long and the old woman turned on her.

"You. You are the quiet one who speaks to no one. I've heard about you."

It wasn't a question and all Azadah could think to do was nod.

"And no man."

"What makes you say that, mother?" She forced out the words, and it seemed the respectful thing to say.

"Your basket is empty yet."

"Yours is very full." So much so that the woman was badly burdened with it. And then Azadah had an idea. "May I help with yours? Do you have far to go?"

"A sweet girl. But I can only pay a little," the woman eyed her shrewdly.

Azadah knew her clothes were tattered and worn. She had not even dusted them off after rising from the hearth before she rushed out the door.

"Even a pittance would help," she tipped her empty basket as an explanation only then realizing that in her haste she had left all of her money tucked under the third rock from the left of the fireplace. Her pockets were as empty as her basket.

"Let's see how you fare."

And so simply, Azadah fell in with Geti and began helping her with the shopping.

8

———

Chris had seen Azadah run out the door, basket in hand even though she'd already been to the market once this morning. He was now so familiar with her ways that he knew something was deeply wrong, but he'd been ill prepared to follow. His sidearms were spread in pieces before him for cleaning and he was not properly clothed to blend into the city.

By the time guns were assembled and he was dressed, he knew there was no point in attempting to follow. Besides, he and Conway were the only two at the house. He'd sent the other two teams out to scour the streets. Over the last three months they had each built up a circle of friendly contacts and now was the time to tap them— one last shot at Syed.

Conway was on guard.

"Which way did she go?"

"She who?" Conway looked truly perplexed. He scanned out the window, then turned to inspect the rooms. "Oh. Servant girl? No idea. Thataway," he waved a hand toward the city.

Chris stood on the threshold squinting against the burning sun. He couldn't wait to get back to a land where people wore sunglasses. Afghanis never seemed to squint or be bothered by the brightness of the day, and since they were undercover they couldn't either.

Ten minutes. She'd had a head start of under ten minutes. But today was Thursday. That made tonight the end of the work week and tomorrow a day of prayer. It was the biggest market of the week, stretching blocks. It would be packed and he'd have no chance of finding her in the crowd.

The "wrongness" was itching at his intuition. After three months he was shocked she even *could* surprise him. Every gesture, every breath, the quiet hum when she was happy about a task, even the way she looked at him when she didn't think he was watching.

Yet something had grabbed her by the throat. If she were a more effusive woman, he'd have expected an outright scream based on the way she'd fled.

Again he went to step across the threshold, but again he stopped.

He had no way to follow her.

...unless he did.

Chris spun on his heel and dug under the other gear for one of the equipment briefcases and dropped it on the table.

"What the hell, Deuce?"

He ignored Conway. His training said to let her go. She had proven herself too many times for her to be a threat. Besides, if she were betraying them, she would not have acted so obviously out of character.

But the man in him had only found one way to interpret her actions: panic. And she'd become far too important for him not to protect her, or at least try.

He *did* have a way to follow her.

"C'mon! C'mon! C'mon!" The computer was taking forever to boot up.

9

———

AZADAH'S ARMS WERE SOON BURNING WITH THE LOAD SHE'D been given to carry; Geti had seen opportunity and shifted all of the heavy items to Azadah's basket. They moved out beyond the last awning of the market and headed north across the city. No car waited, nor a cart. Though the woman was stout and old, she continued to move steadily along despite her burden.

Not a word had passed between them as they shopped, though Geti had plenty to say to the shopkeepers. "This is for a very special man. A very important man. You must give me your best, but at your best price."

Azadah was at first impressed at the prices Geti could get from the merchants, but soon learned to watch their expressions. Some were cautious men, where others looked eager to curry favor. The more she watched, the more she was convinced that she was right. The "important man" must be Syed Harim Akhram, the Taliban commander for all of Helmand Province.

She must get word back to Two C., but she couldn't think of how. Once she'd seen the man Jaffe on the far side of the market. But his glance had slid right by her without recognition and then he was gone.

Beyond the final awning of the market, the cool morning was made hot by the bright sun. She glanced up at the sky, a hazy blue that—

The sky!

Somewhere up there—

She turned her face upward as if warming it in the sun's rays for as long as she dared. She did this again at each turning as they crossed the city.

Now she could only hope.

10

CHRIS SCROLLED BACK TEN MINUTES AND THEN ZOOMED THE recording of the drone's data feed on their little house.

Nothing. Nothing. Nothing. At five minutes he knew he'd missed her. He'd spent too long in indecision.

He rolled backwards faster and faster.

At seventeen minutes back, he found her.

He began scrolling forward at two times speed.

She had rushed out the door. In accelerated mode she practically flew.

He lost her several times with the joystick because when she turned the corner of the street and was out of sight of the house, she'd run as if the very devil was after her.

Chris finally had to slow down the feed while he was still fourteen minutes behind her because she'd reached the edge of the market. Finally he had to go back to real time and growl in frustration at being stuck fourteen minutes behind her actual actions.

Had it not been for her head scarf, he'd never have

been able to track her at all. But the summer green stood out in a sea of blues, grays, and blacks. There were a few scarves that were sunshine yellow and others were ornately decorated, but none like hers.

Besides, now that he was again watching her at normal speed, he'd know it was her anywhere. He'd watched her in the market before when she didn't know he'd spotted her. She walked with her head up and a confidence in her stride that she kept carefully hidden at the house, but was still completely her. All he had to do was watch for a woman who walked like she was the embodiment of summer.

She disappeared beneath an awning and he was momentarily stumped. Then he zoomed back just enough for the edges of the awning to show to all sides of the computer screen.

There!

Crossing the gap between the first stall and the next to the north.

She was moving in no pattern he could detect. It was hard to tell, even at maximum resolution, but her basket appeared to still be empty.

Then she was under one broad awning for so long he was afraid he'd missed her. Just as he was about to scroll back, she stepped once more across a gap. This time she had something in her basket and she was accompanied by another scarf-clad woman. It was the first time he'd ever seen her with another person since—

"Think she's selling us out?"

"Shit!" Chris jumped at finding Conway leaning in over his shoulder to stare at the screen. He'd hit the joystick hard and swung the view several streets to the side. "Damn it, Con Man! No, I don't."

"Jumpy, Deuce. You that hot for the old biddy?"

Chris looked up at him. The man hadn't even looked closely enough to see the beautiful woman hiding in their midst.

Hiding.

What if Conway was right and he was wrong? What if—

"Shut up! Go away!"

Conway shrugged, "Nothing better to do. Jaffe and Maxwell are back. Didn't find shit. So I put them on guard. Better find her again."

Chris kept his snarl to himself. He didn't even know where he'd lost her because he'd been following stall to stall, not going down the street. By the time he located her again, he was over nineteen minutes behind.

He again found where she picked up the companion —older companion by how she moved.

Soon they were both heavily burdened and had exited the market...to the north.

"That's sure not the way back to us," Conway had sat down close beside him.

It wasn't and he was worrying at it when he saw Azadah pause.

She paused...and turned her face to the sky.

It was the moment that had captivated him three long months ago.

But they can see us? She'd asked as she looked for a drone that a very smart woman had known was above them.

Her face then had been so clear. Lit by the sun, her skin had a luminosity that made a man want to kneel before it. That was the moment he would always count as their first meeting. Not when he'd tricked her into speaking Dari, but when he'd seen her face kissed by the sun.

Even though the camera resolution wasn't high enough, his memory was able to easily paint her expression upon the screen.

Do you see me, Two C.? Look, Two C., I'm right here.

He followed the two women up the street. Now that they'd left the covering of the market, it was easy to regain some of the lost minutes on her.

At the next turn, she looked once more to the sky. She looked directly at the drone, her face square into the camera, even though she couldn't possibly know exactly where it was.

He could almost hear her begging him to follow.

"Call everyone in. This is our shot."

Conway didn't move from his side, but was now watching him rather than the small computer screen.

"Trust me. Go."

11

———

"She helped you carry groceries?" The guard hadn't pointed his AK-47 right at her, but it was loose in his hands.

"Yes. A very nice girl. Now pay her fifty Afghanis and she'll be on her way."

The guard reached out a big hand and yanked back the scarf that Azadah had pulled forward as they'd approached.

"Kurdish," he cursed studying her face. "A long way from home, girl." He kept his hand clamped in her hair forcing her to raise her chin. "You spy for Americans or Iranians?"

Geti squinted up at her face and Azadah could see the suspicion forming in the old woman's eyes. Azadah knew it would be a mistake to protest her innocence, but she couldn't think of what else to do. She had to get away, but there was no way to do so without raising more suspicions. So, she'd make up something else.

"For fifty more Afghanis, I will help you cook,

mother," she addressed the woman, though the guard still had her head wrenched back. A hundred was a full day's wages. "For even twenty. My basket was as empty as my belly."

"I think she'd do better waiting with me," the guard shifted his grip to clamping onto her neck in a suggestive way.

"You!" She slapped at his chest. "You unhand this innocent woman. I am for the man who marries me, not someone like you." And when she imagined this man touching her rather than Two C., who had never touched her at all, she couldn't stand it. Acid surged in her belly and she pulled back and spat in the man's face.

His hand struck her so fast that she never saw it coming. She was sprawled in the dirt and all she could think through the slashing pain was that the vegetables and meat she had carried were going to spoil in the hot sand. She tried to gather them up even though she could barely see through the pain and flashes of light.

12

"GOD DAMN IT!" CHRIS WATCHED THE SLAP SEND AZADAH flying.

He bolted up off his chair and would have knocked the laptop to the floor if Conway hadn't grabbed it.

Chris yanked out his sidearm and looked around, but there was no one to shoot. She wasn't here. That goddamn bastard guard—who was going to die slowly, painfully, and begging for mercy from a god he'd never see because he'd roast in hell even if Chris had to escort him there personally—wasn't here either.

"Look."

He did. And all he saw were four dirty walls, too much gear, and no Azadah.

"Look," Conway repeated and tapped the screen.

Chris knew he was being a fool. He slammed his sidearm back in its holster and was now looking over Conway's shoulder.

Slowly, painfully, Azadah was gathering up the shopping items that had been spilled out of her basket.

There was a lot of food there. The second woman was facing off the guard who was actually the one backing away, and her basket wasn't empty either. Then the older woman began helping Azadah refill her basket, climb to her feet, and then led her through the gate.

The moment before she stepped inside the house, Azadah didn't take one last look at the guard. She took one last look at the sky.

And then was gone from the screen.

13

Azadah wished she had made different choices.

Wished she hadn't paid the bribe to get the job of cooking and cleaning for the Americans. Wished she hadn't helped them. Wished she hadn't befriended Geti in the market. And wished she hadn't spit in the guard's face. Already her left eye was swelling shut as Geti tut-tutted about the kitchen and then smeared on a cool salve against the rising heat.

"Nice to see a girl with character. Not very common anymore. Women bareheaded in public. I don't like it. The western music they play. I like that not at all."

Azadah reached up and felt her own bare head, then slid her hand down to her neck where the brute of a guard had grabbed her. No scarf. Her mother's scarf, the last she had of her family's possessions was gone. It was—

"Here you are," Geti's hands were gentle as she lifted the green scarf and wrapped it carefully about Azadah's head.

Even the lightest touch of cloth had her hissing in pain, but she didn't pull away.

"I could use the help and I don't think Mahmood is going to like it if you try to leave."

Once again she had been trapped. Successive cages had driven her south, except beyond Lashkar Gah there had been nowhere else to go. To the south lay only Dasht-e-Margow, the "Desert of Death."

So Azadah did what she must do; as she had so many times before.

She must survive.

She went to her basket and began sorting through the goods and dusting off the sand.

14

———

"It's a goddamn fortress," Conway leaned against the hood of their white Corolla. They had driven by it once which let them view three sides and were now parked a kilometer away where field became hard desert and there was no one to overhear them. In the heat of the day there wasn't even anyone to see them.

Baxter and Burton had passed by the back the compound in a small delivery truck and nodded in agreement.

"We only saw the one guard earlier."

"Now there are ten."

"And that's only outside the wall."

"What about air support?"

Chris shook his head. "No available helicopters. No additional teams either. They've got a big push going against a Taliban training camp and ammunition supply chain up by Khost. All they can offer us is a C-130."

"A Spooky?" Conway sounded excited. A "Spooky" was one of the awe-inspiring gunships in the American arsenal. It could level the compound in minutes with pinpoint accuracy from thousands of feet up, or it could cut a hole in the wall and not touch the building.

"Nope. Cargo. On the ground in Kabul so they need two hours notice to get here."

"So it's just the six of us, one cargo plane, and a pile of bad guys."

"Don't forget the drone." The BB team put in. "Four Hellfires aboard." "Punch an awesome hole." "Delivered and done."

Chris sagged against the hood, and then jolted upright because the metal had become scorching hot under the sun.

"There's a civilian in there."

"Sure, cooks, servants, probably a couple of wives or whores," Conway shrugged. "This is a major meeting. We got to take them out."

Chris groaned and scowled at the ground. It's exactly what Washington was pushing him to do. They hadn't spotted Syed yet. Because Chris didn't trust what Washington would tell him, he had Jaffe and Maxwell back at the house watching the camera feed.

No one doubted Syed would come. It looked as if he was coming to anoint the already-gathering next tier of Taliban leadership to replace those his team had spent the last three months removing. There hadn't been a target like this since the Al-Shabaab training camp in Somalia when a hundred and fifty fighters had been taken down in a single raid.

Washington pushing? Hell! They were going to order an airstrike the minute they confirmed Syed's arrival.

"I repeat, there's a civilian in there." Chris pictured Azadah's last pleading look to the sky as if begging him to come find her.

"What? Our maid?" Conway turned on him. "You're fucking worried about a nobody maid when we've got Syed in our sights?" Then he got a look in his eye. "I *knew* the bitch was putting out for you. Stingy bastard, Deuce, not sharin—"

Chris had never struck a fellow soldier before, but he didn't even think. Conway was four inches taller and several inches broader than he was and Chris laid him out in the dirt.

BB grabbed either of his arms, but he wasn't on the attack. This wasn't some battle.

Conway shook his head trying to clear it and then glared up at him from the dirt.

Chris shrugged and Baxter and Burton let him go but stayed close enough to grab him again if needed.

"Go ahead," Conway turned and spat some blood into the dust. "Deny it. You want to blow off a major kill for bit of stuff."

Chris ignored him and looked to the sky. Just as Azadah had, seeking the drone. Seeking an answer. Seeking help.

"That 'bit of stuff'—who I never touched by the way, asshole—gave us Abdullah. She gave us Majeed, Patris, Wais, and Temur. And now she's given us Syed." Then he looked back down at his teammates. "And if we don't have a better plan ready to go on a moment's notice, Washington is going to pay her back with a one-way ticket to hell."

"She did? The maid was your contact?" Conway stared up at him in shock. "You always had the best leads and none of us ever knew how."

It was more like he was her contact. It was her need to cleanse the land and he had become her instrument of destruction.

"So, we need a plan and we need it fast." He offered a hand to Conway and dragged him up off the dirt. By the strength of their shared handclasp, he knew they were square.

This time it was Conway who looked to the sky, "How long can you hold off Washington?"

"Not very."

"Then," Conway looked down at him and offered the evil smile that had made him Chris' right-hand man for so many tours. "How do you feel about car bombs?"

Chris thought about it for a moment, "Do I have to be driving it when it goes off?"

Conway slapped him on the shoulder and they headed back toward their camp.

15

By the time everything was in place, night had fallen. The temperature was down into the breathable eighties and Chris was sweating more than he did standing out in the midday sun. Dry lightning crackled over the city as it so often did—bright flashes, sharp cracks, and no promise of rain.

He sat at the wheel of the Corolla four blocks and one turn from the terrorists' compound and wished there was a different solution.

But then, as he waited, he could feel the operation-mode take over. There was no past or future within the heart of an operation—only the moment.

For the third time in the last hour his radio crackled to life. "White SUV inbound."

The last two had driven by and continued on into the heart of the city. The compound lay at the end of Lashkargah 2 Road at the north edge of the city. Like most Afghan cities, Lashkar Gah didn't peter out. There were houses crowded together, only distinguishable by their differing styles of protective walls and the color of the door, and then the city ended. The compound was an anomaly, almost as assuredly as bin Laden's massive compound had been. They'd had twenty SEALs, a half dozen helos, and no friendlies inside. He had half a dozen Delta Force operators and—

"Chain of SUVs. Counting five," the drone's pilot reported. With only the six of them, Chris had needed every asset on the ground. He hated depending on some fool with his butt parked in a Nevada bunker, but didn't have a choice.

"Arriving at compound. Unloading. Count twenty-two additional on the ground."

He could practically hear Conway swearing somewhere in the distance. Six Delta and now over forty armed bad guys.

"Syed Harim Akhram confirmed. I repeat. Syed Harim Akhram confirmed."

Past thinking, Chris dropped into gear and put his foot down on the gas.

He heard Conway's radio call of "Friendlies in the compound" that would delay Washington long enough for it to be true. Hopefully. If not, he and the Hellfire missiles should arrive at about the same time.

Four blocks. The engine groaned and the suspension wallowed, but the tough little car began accelerating.

First gear, then he finally nursed the overloaded Corolla into second.

Turning the corner, he had three straight blocks with the compound's gate in full view. Perhaps he'd have another block before the guards heard the straining engine.

Maxwell had cut the power to the local neighborhood at sunset, carefully leaving the compound lit. That way there would be no lights shining on him, but no suspicions raised prematurely.

If he was lucky, maybe they wouldn't see him for two of the three remaining blocks.

He wasn't paying enough attention and hit a pothole. For a second he was afraid he'd broken the frame and their plans would die right here. But it held and the car continued accelerating despite the extra thousand pounds of cargo.

He cursed that cruise controls wouldn't engage until a car was going thirty miles an hour. He was less than half a block from the gates when he hit the thirty-minimum speed.

The first spray of bullets from the gate guard shattered the windshield.

Chris hit the headlights on high-beam and saw the guards raise arms to shield their eyes. It gave him a moment to latch the hook over the steering wheel to hold it on course.

Jaffe had pre-rigged the driver's door so that when Chris pulled the handle, it didn't open—it fell off completely.

One last check...a hundred feet to go...he rolled out of the car and slammed into the ground hard. He spun and slid a dozen yards, almost missing his planned hide.

He dove behind the low wall at the same moment the

plunger detonators on the front of the car hit the main gate.

A thousand pounds of fertilizer taken from agricultural sheds, diesel siphoned from one of the many disabled trucks at the airport, and most of their supply of C-4 exploded.

A blinding sheet of white filled the sky like midday and reflected off the surrounding buildings. The shock wave came next and the low wall collapsed on him.

Too wound up to know if he was hurt, Chris jumped to his feet just as BB crashed their car into two guards who'd somehow survived the initial blast.

Conway drove by in a heavy truck. He slowed just enough for Chris to grab onto the back and be dragged into the bed by Maxwell and Jaffe.

They plowed blindly through the fire that had once been the front gate and a Toyota Corolla. The truck dove into the explosion crater, but was big and powerful enough to bridge over and come out the other side. Conway skidded them to a stop in the forecourt.

Chris went over the top of the cab and the other two guys jumped off the sides.

Anyone who moved received a pair of bullets in the center of their chest and another in the face.

Soon the yard was clear, but the gates had been stout enough that the building still stood intact, except for shattered windows. Gunfire began slashing down at them as BB dove through the flames and added their own guns to the fray.

16

Azadah tried to make sense of what had happened. One moment she was ladling bata rice with a spinach qorma for the guards, including the bastard who had struck her. The next moment she had once again been slammed to the ground.

She lay there wondering who had struck her this time.

No one moved toward her.

Now Mahmood lay near her on the floor as did others.

The air was thick with dust and the room looked as if a whirlwind had blown in the front doors and out the back. The electric lights were gone, but the fire still burned and lit the room, giving the dust a ruddy glow of eternal flames.

Geti had been in the kitchen doorway and now lay far across the room in a position that said she would never rise again.

And then Azadah knew.

She sat up and her head spun no more than it had since Mahmood's earlier blow.

She had not been hit.

Chris had come.

He had seen her pleadings to the sky and he had come for her. Two C. was the soldier she held at a distance with his nickname, but now the man had come for her and earned his true name in her thoughts.

As her hearing recovered, she heard the sounds of gunfire.

So did Mahmood and the other guards. Groping for their weapons, they scrambled to their feet.

No!

She was convinced in that moment Mahmood would kill Chris and she would not let that happen. She swung her ladle and caught him on the side of the face.

He yelped, then turned to face her. Surprise shifted to anger as he struck out at her. Having regained her feet, she was able to duck his first blow. Then she was aware of the iron pot still in her other hand.

Swinging it with all of her might, she slammed it into the side of head.

He staggered for a moment, dazed.

This time she spun fully around until she needed both hands to hold the pot against its desire to fly away. It smashed into the side of his head, shattering his cheek and jaw.

Still he stood.

The ladle gone, the pot snatched from her hands by the force of impact, she grabbed for the long kitchen knife on the table.

Then Mahmood twitched...and dropped to the floor like a sack of grain.

Only as he fell did she see two holes had appeared in his chest.

She spun to the face the back door.

There, on the threshold, was an apparition. A brief flash of lightning silhouetted Chris kneeling in the doorway, his rifle spitting fire.

His face lit green by the light of his night-vision goggles, Chris was shooting at the other guards in the room so quickly it might have been a single barrage, but it wasn't. In slow motion she could see each time he pulled the trigger. Could hear the bullets whistle past her. One tugged at her dress. But it wasn't a miss. Each shot was followed by the slap of bullet striking flesh behind her. Each grunt, the last gasp of a man already dead, but not yet fallen.

She turned, safe in the midst of the cloud of death, and watched the men fall until there were only the two of them in the room.

Chris rushed up to her.

He didn't take her in his arms.

He didn't kiss her madly as she had dreamed so many nights while sitting beside him under the stars.

When she looked at his eyes illuminated by the green glow of his goggles, she saw a hard man there. Yet this man she knew as well. This was Deuce, the seasoned fighter. The one she had seen him shed slowly, after each operation, over the last three months as he turned back into Chris.

"Take my belt. Hold hard. Do exactly what I do and

don't let go. I have a tag-a-long," he spoke as if to someone else.

Oh. Warning the others over the radio not to shoot the person at his back.

Then he stepped by her as if he'd forgotten she was there.

17

———

CHRIS FELT THE REASSURING TUG ON THE BACK OF HIS BELT and then focused on what he had to do.

There was a dancelike flow to room-clearing. Six Delta operators hitting a target so hard, so fast, that there was no time for others to react.

The radio was no more than the occasional dance of positional calls. "B-1-3." Someone from his team—it didn't matter who—was about to enter through the third window of the first floor on the "B" side of the building—the second counting clockwise from the "A" front.

Chris called "B-1-3 inside" and the two of them entered from opposite directions safe from each other's field of fire. In five seconds there were no unfriendlies left standing in the room.

Together they moved back along the B-wall, dropping two more guards, until they had cleared the other rooms up to "A."

"Two in five seconds, A and C," Some part of him registered a BB voice. They'd found a way to scale the building and were hitting the second floor front and back.

He and Conway surged for the front stairs. Maxwell and Jaffe were prone at opposite corners of the yard offering sniper coverage as well as targeting anyone who tried to run from the building.

18

Azadah felt as if she was being sucked along by a whirlwind.

Not once did Chris run. Instead he crouched slightly and flowed down the hall, gliding up the stairs as fast as rising smoke. By her hand wrapped hard around his belt, she could feel the perfect steadiness of his torso despite how fast his legs were moving.

In the front of the house, a raging fire shone in through the windows. Then they would plunge into an interior room and she'd be blind in the darkness except for the bright flashes from Chris' or another's weapons.

This must be how a child feels in the womb. Safe, unaware. Following in the wake of the mother/protector's every move.

It was as if she and Chris had become one. He would pause, step, turn, fire, move. She would pause, step, turn, watch another fall, move.

A room with too many to fight. They ducked back out

of sight as bullets streamed forth and struck the wall opposite the doorway.

Chris slid something from his waist and tossed it into the room.

A blinding stream of light shone out, illuminating the bullet-ridden wall in stark relief, and then a shuddering bang of sound so loud that her ears ached in the hallway outside the room.

Now she knew what to do and was already rising as Chris flowed forward once more, clearing the room rapidly, each with three spits from his quiet gun.

A sudden stillness descended around them.

There was no more gunfire.

No flashes of light in the night. Now only the fire lit the rooms.

Azadah looked about. They were in a bedroom that had once been luxurious. A shattered mirror clung to a gold-painted frame big enough for two people to see themselves in. A bed of dark wood had three bodies lying upon it, their blood slowly masking the fine needlework of the spread.

Close beside her, the door of an armoire, struck with two bullets, slowly swinging open.

Out of it, the muzzle of a gun emerging.

Too late for Chris to turn.

Too late to pull him aside by the hand wrapped so firmly about his belt that she could hope it would never come free.

In her other hand...the kitchen knife.

With a swing, she sliced the blade upward in the slot.

Impact.

A cry.

The gun dropping.

And Chris' handgun firing inches from her face.

Not two shots, not three.

He emptied the entire magazine into the cabinet.

19

———

CHRIS HOLSTERED HIS SIDEARM AND NUDGED THE DOOR open with the muzzle of his rifle.

A man slumped out of the cabinet and onto the floor.

"Syed," Azadah breathed close by his shoulder. Of course, she must have seen the files he and his men had been studying.

"A bit of overkill, Deuce," Conway observed as he joined them and looked down at the body.

At least a dozen shots had hit him. Face, chest, neck. There was also a nasty gash on his arm, the single slice with which Azadah had saved his life.

"We clear?"

"Roger that."

Chris looked at his watch. He wanted to comfort Azadah. Make sure she was unhurt. He wanted to tell her things that a man only ever told one woman.

But there wasn't time.

"Five minutes. Gather intel, then we're gone."

"Roger that."

As Chris moved about the house, he was aware of the slight pressure against the small of his back. The connection through which he and Azadah had moved in such perfect harmony.

They took wallets and shot photographs. They smashed laptops and wrenched out hard drives to shove into pockets. Cell phones and USBs were gathered, but there was too much. Conway stuffed rolls of maps into a blood-stained pillowcase. Baxter and Burton slammed paper files into knapsacks.

The five minutes seemed to slide by in seconds.

Inside the front door he called over the radio, "Four —" the pressure at his waist, "Five coming out."

"Roger," Jaffe's promise that he wouldn't shoot them as they exited the building.

"Hoof it!" They raced across the forecourt, picked up the two outside men, and the seven of them dodged through the remnants of fire at the front gate. Circling the building, they sprinted across the field and headed for the open desert.

"Drone pilot, we're clear. Repeat ground team is clear. You may fire at will."

If Azadah was flagging, she didn't indicate it. She remained his shadow across the fields as if they were one united body.

There was a high shriek from above and a streak of light across the desert sky.

20

——————

It was as bright as a lightning bolt heaved from the heavens, but straight as an arrow.

Azadah could not see the ground at her feet and could only rely on her contact with Chris to lead her to safety.

She turned her head enough to watch the lightning bolt as it struck down behind them. A ball of fire erupted back toward the heavens. Only the wall that encircled the compound kept her from being blinded.

Hellfire.

That is what the Americans had sent down on Syed's grave.

A Hellfire missile.

It was what he'd deserved.

It would hide the team's actions, for they were the silent warriors. Now it would be just another drone strike with another set of confirmed kills—confirmed by those who had already pulled the triggers before vanishing into the night.

When the rolling thunder washed over her, she looked from the fire to the men who ran near her. They had done as Chris had promised; they had returned and cut the head off the snake. Yes, it would be born anew, but it would not happen soon or well after such a blow.

Chris came to a halt and so did she. She was gasping for air, but had never felt so alive in her life.

The others gathered around and they were all watching the sky.

After the brightness of the explosion she could see nothing. Then a brief lightning flash from the dwindling storm revealed a great plane descending out of the night sky.

Chris reached back and took her hand as he turned to face her. It was stiff with being clenched so long about his belt, upon her scarf when she slept, on the last shreds of her very existence. He massaged it back to life. He slid up his night-vision gear and she could just make out his face in the light of the dying fire now a kilometer behind them across the dry grass.

"Azadah," her name was a whisper on his breath. "This plane will not land again in Afghanistan."

She felt a sudden chill. He couldn't be saying goodbye. Not here. Not after all they had been through together.

"If you step on this plane…" but he stopped.

A whisper of hope was caught in the desert wind and fluttered aloft for a moment, but faded away as he remained silent.

"Please," he started again. "Please come with me."

And born once more here in the cool air of the Afghan night, she faced him.

"I would show you my house..." Chris again fell silent.

And after being so long silent, her voice unlocked as if it had never been frozen. And the question that slid out was of her heart's making, not her mind's. "Tell me, Chris..."

And he waited for the words to fill the tiny space between them as the giant plane touched down in the desert and rolled toward them.

"Tell me that together we will make it a *home* and then I will go with you."

He brushed his hand so gently along her injured cheek that she felt no pain. "There is no greater gift you could give me," and he smiled at her.

And she knew he spoke truth, for that was the man he was.

The others were already up the ramp, but she halted one step from the clean steel slope. She thought of all the past and all the pain. Somehow it had lead to this incredible moment.

Azadah looked one last time at a night sky of emerging stars she would forever own as she stepped off a desert she would never see again.

Her home was in the heart of a man. This man. The one she would always walk beside no matter where the path lay.

For there was no greater gift than this man who had come to her from the sky.

LAST WORDS

I hope that you enjoyed this journey through the land of my Delta Force Shooter romance stories.

I've written other tales of Delta Force for other reasons, and I've gathered those in a separate collection.

Having walked this road, I feel that I've gained more personal understanding of what drives people to a career that I didn't choose, and probably could not have tolerated even if I had.

I am not like these warriors.

But neither are they "other."

They are people who have chosen a path. Ones who do their absolute best, under unimaginably difficult circumstances, to do the right thing for the right reasons.

I can only hope that I've captured even a glimmer of who they are with my stories.

And I so loved giving them the happy endings they deserve.

Thank you for joining me.

Aim high!

M. L. Buchman

North Shore, MA 2020

IF YOU ENJOYED THAT,

BE SURE YOU DON'T MISS THE MIRANDA CHASE SERIES!

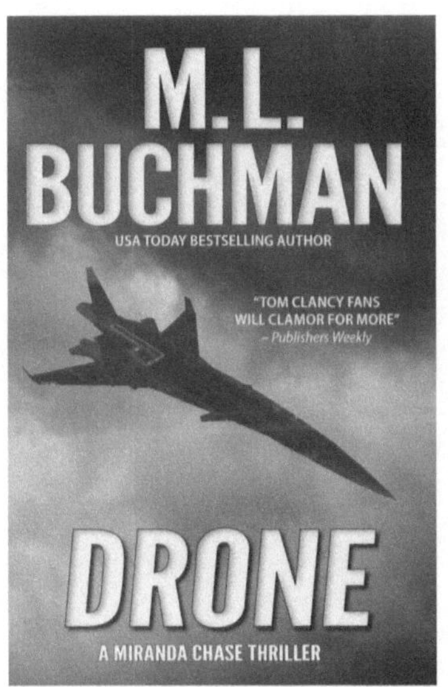

DRONE (EXCERPT)

Flight 630 at 37,000 feet
12 nautical miles north of
Santa Fe, New Mexico, USA

THE FLIGHT ATTENDANT STEPPED UP TO HER SEAT—4E—which had never been her favorite on a 767-300. At least the cabin setup was in the familiar 261-seat, 2-class configuration, currently running at a seventy-three percent load capacity with a standard crew of ten and one ride-along FAA inspector in the cockpit jump seat.

"Excuse me, are you Miranda Chase?"

She nodded.

The attendant made a face that she couldn't interpret.

A frown? Did that indicate anger?

He turned away before she could consider the possibilities and, without another word, returned to his station at the front of the cabin.

Miranda once again straightened the emergency exit plan that the flight's vibrations kept shifting askew in its pocket.

This flight from yesterday's meeting at LAX to today's DC lunch meeting at the National Transportation Safety Board's headquarters departed so early that she'd decided to spend the night in the airline's executive lounge working on various aviation accident reports. She never slept on a flight and would have to catch up on her sleep tonight.

Miranda felt the shift as the plane turned into a modest five-degree bank to the left. The bright rays of dawn over the New Mexico desert shifted from the left-hand windows to the right side.

At due north, she heard the Rolls-Royce RB211 engines (quite a pleasant high tone compared to the Pratt & Whitney PW4000 that she always found unnerving) ease off ever so slightly, signaling a slow descent. The pilot was transitioning from an eastbound course that would be flown at an odd number of thousands of feet to a westbound one that must be flown at an even number.

The flight attendant then picked up the intercom phone and a loud squawk sounded through the cabin. Most people would be asleep and there were soft complaints and rustling down the length of the aircraft.

"We regret to inform you that there is an emergency on the ground. I repeat, there is nothing wrong with the plane. We are being routed back to Las Vegas, where we will disembark one passenger, refuel, and then continue our flight to DC. Our apologies for the inconvenience."

There were now shouts of complaint all up and down the aisle.

The flight attendant was staring straight at her as he slammed the intercom back into its cradle with significantly greater force than was required to seat it properly.

Oh. It was her they would be disembarking. That meant there was a crash in need of an NTSB investigator —a major one if they were flying back an hour in the wrong direction.

Thankfully, she always had her site kit with her.

For some reason, her seatmate was muttering something foul. Miranda ignored it and began to prepare herself.

Only the crash mattered.

She straightened the exit plan once more. It had shifted the other way with the changing harmonic from the RB211 engines.

———

Chengdu, Central China

Air Force Major Wang Fan eased back on the joystick of the final prototype Shenyang J-31 jet— designed exclusively for the People's Liberation Army Air Force. In response, China's newest fighter jet leapt upward like a catapult's missile from the PLAAF base in the flatlands surrounding the towering city of Chengdu.

It felt as he'd just been grasped by Chen Mei-Li. Never had a woman made him feel so much like a man.

———

Keep reading at fine retailers everywhere:
Drone

ABOUT THE AUTHOR

USA Today and Amazon #1 Bestseller M. L. "Matt" Buchman started writing on a flight south from Japan to ride his bicycle across the Australian Outback. Just part of a solo around-the-world trip that ultimately launched his writing career.

From the very beginning, his powerful female heroines insisted on putting character first, *then* a great adventure. He's since written over 60 action-adventure thrillers and military romantic suspense novels. And just for the fun of it: 100 short stories, and a fast-growing pile of read-by-author audiobooks.

Booklist says: "3X Top 10 of the Year." PW says: "Tom Clancy fans open to a strong female lead will clamor for more." His fans say: "I want more now...of everything." That his characters are even more insistent than his fans is a hoot.

As a 30-year project manager with a geophysics degree who has designed and built houses, flown and jumped out of planes, and solo-sailed a 50' ketch, he is awed by what is possible. More at: www.mlbuchman.com.

Other works by M. L. Buchman: *(* - also in audio)*

Thrillers

Dead Chef
One Chef!
Two Chef!

Miranda Chase
*Drone**
*Thunderbolt**
*Condor**
*Ghostrider**

Romantic Suspense

Delta Force
*Target Engaged**
*Heart Strike**
*Wild Justice**
*Midnight Trust**

Firehawks
MAIN FLIGHT
Pure Heat
Full Blaze
*Hot Point**
*Flash of Fire**
Wild Fire
SMOKEJUMPERS
*Wildfire at Dawn**
*Wildfire at Larch Creek**
*Wildfire on the Skagit**

The Night Stalkers
MAIN FLIGHT
The Night Is Mine
I Own the Dawn
Wait Until Dark
Take Over at Midnight
Light Up the Night
Bring On the Dusk
By Break of Day

AND THE NAVY
Christmas at Steel Beach
Christmas at Peleliu Cove
WHITE HOUSE HOLIDAY
*Daniel's Christmas**
*Frank's Independence Day**
*Peter's Christmas**
*Zachary's Christmas**
*Roy's Independence Day**
*Damien's Christmas**
5E
Target of the Heart
Target Lock on Love
Target of Mine
Target of One's Own

Shadow Force: Psi
*At the Slightest Sound**
*At the Quietest Word**

White House Protection Force
*Off the Leash**
*On Your Mark**
*In the Weeds**

Contemporary Romance

Eagle Cove
Return to Eagle Cove
Recipe for Eagle Cove
Longing for Eagle Cove
Keepsake for Eagle Cove

Henderson's Ranch
*Nathan's Big Sky**
*Big Sky, Loyal Heart**
*Big Sky Dog Whisperer**

Love Abroad
Heart of the Cotswolds: England
Path of Love: Cinque Terre, Italy

Other works by M. L. Buchman:

Contemporary Romance (cont)

Where Dreams
Where Dreams are Born
Where Dreams Reside
Where Dreams Are of Christmas
Where Dreams Unfold
Where Dreams Are Written

Science Fiction / Fantasy

Deities Anonymous
Cookbook from Hell: Reheated
Saviors 101

Single Titles
The Nara Reaction
Monk's Maze
the Me and Elsie Chronicles

Non-Fiction

Strategies for Success
Managing Your Inner Artist/Writer
Estate Planning for Authors
Character Voice

Short Story Series by M. L. Buchman:

Romantic Suspense

Delta Force
Delta Force

Firehawks
The Firehawks Lookouts
The Firehawks Hotshots
The Firebirds

The Night Stalkers
The Night Stalkers
The Night Stalkers 5E
The Night Stalkers CSAR
The Night Stalkers Wedding Stories

US Coast Guard
US Coast Guard

White House Protection Force
White House Protection Force

Contemporary Romance

Eagle Cove
Eagle Cove

Henderson's Ranch
Henderson's Ranch

Where Dreams
Where Dreams

Thrillers

Dead Chef
Dead Chef

Science Fiction / Fantasy

Deities Anonymous
Deities Anonymous

Other
The Future Night Stalkers
Single Titles

SIGN UP FOR M. L. BUCHMAN'S NEWSLETTER TODAY

and receive:
Release News
Free Short Stories
a Free Book

Get your free book today. Do it now.
free-book.mlbuchman.com